THE MYSTERY
OF BRISTLECONE PINE

LASSIE

THE MYSTERY
OF BRISTLECONE PINE

AUTHORIZED EDITION

by STEVE FRAZEE

Cover illustration by
ROD RUTH

Illustrated by
LARRY HARRIS

GOLDEN PRESS
Western Publishing Company, Inc.
Racine, Wisconsin

© MCMLXVII, MCMLXXIX Lassie Television, Inc.
All rights reserved.

Produced in U.S.A. by
Western Publishing Company, Inc.
Racine, Wisconsin

GOLDEN® and GOLDEN PRESS® are registered
trademarks of Western Publishing Company, Inc.

No part of this book may be reproduced or
copied in any form without written permission
from the publisher.

0-307-21505-9

Contents

1 Fire!   7

2 Fight!   19

3 Sheriff Sam   34

4 The Red Devils   49

5 The Gunfighters   64

6 Friendly Enemies   79

7 The Searchers   96

8 Danger Trail   112

9 A Confession   126

10 An Angry Bear   140

11 Logging Camp   155

12 Discoveries   169

13 The Last Trip   185

14 Gallant Swimmer   199

Riding with Ranger Corey Stuart in the green Forest Service Jeep, Lassie began to whine anxiously as they started down the steep grade of Sawmill Hill near Cyclone Creek.

"What is it, Lassie?" Corey asked. He was a tall, trimly built man with a face heavily tanned by long exposure to wind and sun. The weather creases at the corners of his eyes crinkled as he looked inquiringly at the big gold and white collie.

It was only a quick glance because he had to keep his eyes on the narrow, plunging road—little more than a horse trail, really. Tall blue spruces grew thickly on both sides of the road, their branch tips silvery with new growth.

Lassie continued to whine; she was standing now as she looked over the side of the Jeep.

An elk, perhaps, Corey thought. There were plenty of them in the area. He had seen a big herd of them during the two days he had spent at Cyclone Peak guard station.

Lassie continued to whine, and finally Corey stopped the Jeep. She leaped out at once and went running down into the trees. It was not the sight of an animal that was troubling her, Corey knew. She had seen too many of them to get excited about them, and she had been trained long before not to chase them.

He waited, looking down into the trees. A few moments later he heard Lassie barking. It was an angry, warning kind of bark.

Corey started down to her, and then, just below the road, he caught the odor of smoke. Quickly he scrambled back to the Jeep and got a shovel.

As he ran down through the dense growth, the odor of burning wood and pine needles became stronger. And then he saw the smoke, drifting low through the trees. After another hundred feet, he caught a glimpse of flame licking at the forest mat.

Fire! The event most dreaded by a Forest Ranger. For three weeks there had been no rain. Throughout all the Sleepy Cat National Forest the fire danger was high.

Lassie continued to bark. Corey ran faster.

Eighty years before, there had been a sawmill on the creek. If the fire had gotten into the deep scatter of sawdust near the growth of new timber, Corey knew he was in for trouble.

As he burst out of the dense stand of trees he took in the situation with a few quick looks. A campfire had been built in the thick needle mat not far from the creek. It had gotten away and was now spreading rapidly toward the trees.

A skinny, scared-faced boy was standing with his back against a tall stump, a club raised in both hands. Lassie was barking at him from about ten feet away.

"It's all right, Lassie!" Corey said, and he immediately went to work. He dug through the needles down to earth, making a trench all around the perimeter of the fire. On one side the flames had run close to the wind-scattered carpet of sawdust, now brown and rotting from age.

"Get your father!" Corey shouted at the boy, not even pausing in his work.

The boy only glanced at him before looking back at Lassie. He did not move.

"She won't hurt you," Corey said. He finished his trench near the sawdust and ran to the side of the fire where the trees were threatened. For a while it was a close race, and then he saw that he had the fire fairly well beaten. He had it contained within the limits of his digging.

Panting hard from the exertion, he removed his safety hat and wiped his brow. The boy was still backed against the stump, his eyes on Lassie. The collie was lying down, watching him.

"Where're your parents, son?"

The boy shook his head sullenly.

"Well, who is with you?"

"Nobody," the boy said.

He was about twelve, Corey thought, thin-faced and big-eyed, a bit on the scrawny side. His dark hair was sticking out from under a cowboy hat that had once been white. His jeans were torn and filthy, and his cowboy boots had had hard use.

"You can put the club down, son. Lassie won't bother you."

"She's mean and dangerous!"

"Did you try to hit her with that club?"

"Sure I did! She was going to bite me!"

"Maybe she should have nipped you a little. She doesn't like careless people in the forest any more than I do."

"I tried to put it out," the boy said, "but it kept spreading."

Now that he had time to look, Corey observed that the boy had dug the needle mat away from his fire site, though not far enough. He saw, also, a small frying pan lying near the creek.

"I was carrying water in the frying pan when your old dog came after me."

"Fine!" Corey said. "Now you can carry some more. In my Jeep up there on the road you'll find a folding canvas bucket."

The boy looked at him stubbornly. "You can't make me help you."

"No, I can't, but I think you will."

Lassie was still uneasy about the smoldering fire. She whined, as if to say, "Let's get the job finished."

For the first time Corey saw the camping gear behind the stump. There was a light sleeping bag and a pack. "You walked up here all by yourself?"

"I said so, didn't I?"

Fourteen long, steep miles from Big Sunset, the nearest town. Corey studied the boy closely. "Didn't that chip on your shoulder get a little heavy during your hike?"

"I don't know what you mean."

"Oh?" Corey paused. "How about the bucket?"

The boy met the ranger's steady gaze for a while, and then his eyes dropped. "All right." He walked away, still carrying his club. Corey looked at the run-over heels of his scuffed cowboy boots and shook his head.

Before long the boy was back with the canvas

bucket. He still carried the club. After the second trip to the creek for water, he dropped the weapon.

Corey stirred the smoldering needle mat with the shovel while the boy poured water on it. When it seemed to the boy that they had covered the whole burning area, he tossed the bucket aside.

"Take a rest, if you want to," Corey said, "and then we'll soak it all again just to be sure."

The boy glared at him. "You think you're tough, don't you? Where I come from—" He did not finish.

"Where *do* you come from, Rocky?"

"That isn't my name!"

"What *is* your name?"

The boy licked his lips. His face was begrimed with soot and dirt. A glint of mockery showed in his eyes as he said, "Cone."

"How do you spell that?"

"C-o-n-e! How do you think? Just because I don't wear my name on my shirt pocket like you—"

"Get some more water, C-o-n-e."

Lassie had been rambling about on her own. From a rusting pile of tin cans near the old sawmill cabin she took a coffee can in her teeth and laid it at Cone's feet when he reached the creek. She seemed to be saying, "You can fill this with water."

Cone backed away from her quickly. Lassie picked the can up and came to him again.

"Make her leave me alone!" Cone yelled.

"Come here, Lassie." Corey knew that it was a silly belief that all children and dogs automatically loved each other on sight. They both had to be trained to appreciate and respect each other.

It was very unusual, though, when Lassie could not make friends. Corey guessed that Cone must have had a bad experience with a dog, or maybe he was just naturally afraid of animals.

Lassie brought the can to Corey. When Cone came up from the creek with a partly filled bucket, he said, "She's not very smart, is she? The bottom is almost rusted out of that can."

Corey smiled. "She's smart enough not to start forest fires."

Cone had no more to say after that.

When Corey was sure that the last spark had been soaked with water, he turned to look at the great stretch of timber reaching up the mountain. "What do you think fire would have done to that, Cone?"

The boy shifted his feet uneasily. "I tried to put it out, I said, and then your mean old dog scared me."

"It's easier not to let them start."

"I know. I should have dug all that stuff way back from my campfire, or built it in the sand down there by the creek." For the first time Cone seemed genuinely concerned about what he had done. "What are you going to do to me?"

"Nothing. Gather up your stuff and let's go."

Instantly the boy became wary. "Go where?"

"To town. Big Sunset." As district ranger, Corey had his home and headquarters there. "You came from one of the summer camps down there, didn't you?"

Cone shook his head quickly. "I'm staying here.

I won't start any more fires. I promise."

Corey went over to the stump and picked up the pack. He hefted it by the carrying straps. "I'd say you didn't have three pounds of food in there."

"I've been getting along all right."

Yeah, Corey thought, *dirty, ragged, and half-starved.* "Let's go, Cone."

For a moment Corey thought the boy was going to cry, and then Cone clamped his lips tight and got control of himself. He picked up his frying pan and put it in the pack. "You're going to take me to the station, huh?"

Station? There was no railroad into Big Sunset. Then Corey understood what the boy meant. Police station. "What have you done, Cone, that would make you think that?"

"Nothing! I just—" The boy did not finish.

A runaway, Corey thought. It happened every summer. A boy became homesick or upset about something in one of the summer camps near Long Lake, and then he took off on his own.

Usually, though, they would head for home.

Cone was the first one he had ever known to wind up fourteen miles deep in the Sleepy Cat National Forest.

With Lassie frisking along in front of them, the ranger and the boy went up the hill to the Jeep.

"Which camp are you from?" Corey asked.

The boy shook his head.

"We'll just have to find that out when we get there." Corey put the boy's gear in the backseat, and then he said to Lassie, "Backseat for you, girl. Jump!"

Cone got in front beside Corey. The boy looked over his shoulder at the dog. "She's sure got awful big teeth."

Corey held back a smile. For a few moments he looked down into the trees. A light wind from the west was still blowing. For the most part it had carried the smoke away from the road. Intent as he had been on his driving, Corey knew that he would have gone right on past the fire without knowing about it, if it had not been for Lassie's sensitive nose.

Fifteen minutes more and the thing would have been a raging red monster, devouring everything in its path.

He turned to pat Lassie on the head. "You sure did a job today!"

"Hey! You've got a radio!" Cone said. He watched Corey's moves with interest as the ranger started the engine, released the emergency brake, and eased down the rocky road in four-wheel drive.

"What's your last name?" Corey asked.

The boy hesitated. Glancing sideways, Corey saw his thin face light with an impish expression.

"My last name is Pine."

Cone Pine. Cone Pine. Corey let the name run through his mind several times. He did not get around to reversing the two words until the boy said, "My first name is Bristle."

"Bristlecone Pine. Your name is Bristlecone Pine!"

"Yup," the boy said.

AT THE JUNCTION of Cyclone and Silver Bear Creeks the road forked. The newer and better road ran up Silver Bear for about a mile to where Bo Wilson's loggers were cutting timber.

Corey's assistant, Brad Martin, was the one who usually checked on the timber operation, but for a week now he had been with an erosion control crew in the western part of the forest.

Corey turned up Silver Bear Creek.

He glanced at his passenger. It was the boy's first Jeep ride, he thought, judging from the eager interest Cone had shown in everything about the vehicle.

As they went up the haul road the boy said, "Whoever built this sure didn't know much about making roads."

"How do you mean?"

"All those bumpy dips."

Corey grinned. "Those are water bars. We require them to be put there so the water will run off the road into the trees, instead of building up into a stream and gouging big ruts. If that happens, all you have is a rocky trench."

"Water bars, huh?" Cone seemed to be interested for a moment, and then he said, "Big deal!"

They came to where the timber crew was working in Redmon Basin. Two men with gasoline chain saws were cutting and trimming trees. Bo Wilson, a huge, red-faced man, was running the loader that lifted the logs onto the trucks. When he saw Corey he shut off the engine and leaped down.

"Hiya, Ranger!" Bo shouted, his voice booming. "Who you got with you, a new assistant?"

Corey grinned. "Yes, sir, Bo. This is my new junior forester. He's going to see that you boys don't do any high-stumping or cut way beyond the sale boundary."

Bo laughed. "The trouble with you Forest Service characters is that you're always keeping me honest against my will."

It was a joke between them. Bo Wilson was one logger on the Sleepy Cat whom Corey was always glad to see get a contract. Bo was particular about his roads, and he always lived up to his agreements. He understood the value of the National Forest and its products.

He came stomping over to the Jeep as Corey and the boy got out. Looking at the size of the logger, Cone half-expected the ground to tremble. Lassie had already bounded away and was prowling through the underbrush.

Bo looked Cone over curiously. "You been working in a coal bin somewhere, son?"

"This is—" Corey hesitated. "This is my friend, Briss."

"Hiya, Briss," Bo said, and then he seemed to forget about the boy. "Say, Corey, I'm going to have a little problem with slash there near the creek. Let me show you."

The two men walked away. Briss—he sort of liked that name—went over to the loader. That was some machine! It had lifted a big log on the truck as easy as pie. He wondered how long it would take to learn to operate the loader.

Somewhere over in the woods another piece of heavy equipment was growling. The sound grew louder and then Briss saw a bulldozer coming toward him, dragging three big logs on a chain.

What amazed him was the fact that a boy about his own age was operating the dozer. He was a round-faced, red-headed boy, and he was sitting up there on the dozer as if he owned the whole world.

As the machine came closer, the boy shouted something at Briss and waved his arm. Briss could not hear what he was saying because of the sound of the heavy engine, nor did he understand what the redhead meant by his violent arm signals.

Twenty feet away the boy stopped the dozer and turned off the engine. "For pete's sake, kid, are you too dumb to get out of my way?"

Briss realized then that he was standing right where the boy wanted to drag the logs. He felt foolish as he moved quickly aside.

With Briss out of the way, the dozer operator resumed his work. He sure knew how to handle that machine, Briss thought. A loudmouth, but he sure could run a dozer.

After he had dragged the logs in place and unhooked them, the red-headed boy parked the dozer and cut the engine. He stood up in the seat and called out, "Hey, Uncle Bo, there're your last three logs for the load!"

Bo waved his hand. "Okay, Chub. Help the men load the tools."

There was a swagger in Chub's walk as he came over to Briss. "What are you doing, riding around with the ranger, kid?"

Kid! Briss did not care for the name. Maybe Chub was a little bigger than he was, and could run a dozer, but that was no reason for him to strut around acting important.

"What's your name?" Chub demanded.

"Briss. That's short for Bristlecone Pine, kid."

Chub blinked in surprise. "Yeah?"

"Yeah!"

"Where'd you get that crummy hat?"

"I bought it."

"You found it in a dump, I bet." Chub reached out and snatched the cowboy hat from Briss's head. He examined it, shaking his head. "Boy, is that crummy!" Then he tossed it to the ground.

Corey and Bo were talking near the creek. Lassie was across the stream from them, sniffing around a stump. Suddenly she began to bark. Bo Wilson laughed. "Don't tell me you've got her trained to sniff out stumps more than a foot high."

To avoid waste and to make forest management easier, trees were to be cut no higher than one foot from the ground on the high side. Corey knew that Bo seldom violated the regulation, and he knew that Lassie probably was barking at the entrance of some small animal's burrow near the stump. He grinned and said, "I guess she's caught you this time, Bo." Both men laughed heartily.

Then they noticed that Lassie had forgotten all about the stump. She had bounded across the creek and was racing toward the trucks.

Corey turned his head to watch her, and it was then that he saw the fight.

It had started already, for Briss was just getting up from a sitting position. Punching with both hands, he drove in at Chub. Chub's head rocked back from one of the blows and then he grabbed the smaller boy's arms.

They began to wrestle. Both went to the ground, with Chub on top.

"Stop that!" Corey shouted. He began to run.

Lassie was way ahead of him. She grabbed Chub by the seat of the pants, trying to tug him off Briss. Chub reached back with one hand and tried to push her away. "Let go, you! Lassie, let go!"

Growling and twisting her head, the big collie kept pulling.

Though Briss was flat on his back, he was whacking away with both hands. Trying to push

Lassie away with one hand and protect his face with the other, Chub was having a bad time.

"That's enough, Lassie!" Corey said. He pulled Chub to his feet; then he grabbed Briss and lifted him off the ground.

Chub was willing to let it go, but Briss was all for resuming the scrap. His face was white under the grime. His dark eyes were blazing.

"Whoa, there!" Corey said, dragging him back when he tried to rush at Chub, who was feeling the seat of his pants as he backed away.

To show that there were no hard feelings, Lassie wagged her tail. "You sure can pull, Lassie," Chub told her. He felt his jaw and stared at Briss. "You're kind of a wildcat, aren't you?"

Briss was not one to cool off so readily. He jerked away from Corey and went to the Jeep.

"What's the idea of picking on that skinny kid?" Bo Wilson growled at his nephew. "You think you're a big, tough logger?"

"I didn't pick on him. He belted me first." Chub felt his jaw. "He belts pretty hard, too."

"Serves you right." Bo frowned at Corey. "That's the trouble with trying to raise a kid around a bunch of loggers. He begins to think he's a man, and a prizefighter to boot."

"He hit me first!" Chub protested.

"Aw, beat it," Bo said. "Help the men load the tools."

After Corey and Briss left the loggers, Briss did not talk until long after they had passed the fork of the road. He huddled against his side of the Jeep, now and then turning to look at Lassie with a puzzled expression.

"Chub is a pretty big lad for you to tackle," Corey said.

"I don't care how big he is."

"He's not a bad kid, Briss. When he was just a baby, his parents were killed in a car accident. Bo took him in. Ever since he could walk, he's been going to the woods with Bo in the summer, or hanging around the sawmill. Being with men most of the time that way—"

"He's not so tough." Briss looked at Lassie.

"Why did your dog help me?"

Corey spoke gently. "Because she figured you needed a friend."

"Huh!"

A friend was exactly what the boy needed, Corey thought. Maybe after he got back to the camp and stayed awhile, things would work out for him. "Which one of the camps were you in, Briss?"

"None of them."

Corey sighed. He guessed he had better start finding out the truth about the boy as soon as they reached the Scout's Nest, about four miles down the road.

Unless he was in a hurry because of an emergency, Corey always stopped at Scout's Nest. It was a high point on the rocky shoulder of the mountain. In early days the Indians had posted lookouts there to watch for enemies far below in the valley.

Radio transmission was very good from the point. Also, there was a spring close by that was supposed to have the best-tasting water in the area.

Aside from those facts, the main reason Corey liked to pause at Scout's Nest was to spend a few quiet minutes looking at the vast reaches of the Sleepy Cat National Forest. From this point he could see beyond the Flying Horse Mountains across the valley to other ranges, which were misty with distance.

The little town of Big Sunset was four thousand feet below. From Scout's Nest the houses were tiny and the cars were like small toys. Most of Long Lake was visible; it was now shining in the late afternoon sun clear up to Thunder Narrows, where the water lay between steep cliffs.

"Some view, isn't it, Briss?"

Briss was looking at the town and the lodges and the summer camps scattered along the lakeshore. "Yeah," he said.

"See that rock formation just to the right of the peak with all the snow? That's how the forest got its name."

The boy raised his eyes. For a moment there was interest in his voice as he said, "It sure does look like a snoozing cat." Then his expression was once more tired and unhappy.

"See that shiny thing above the trees way over there on the mountains?" Corey asked.

Briss nodded.

"That's one of our fire lookout towers." Corey took the microphone from its bracket and called the tower.

The lookout answered promptly.

"All clear today, I hope?" Corey asked.

"All clear. At two-oh-three I thought for a while that I saw smoke on Cyclone Creek, but it disappeared before I was sure."

"Campfire. I was there."

The lookout signed off.

"That was a woman!" Briss said. He stared at the distant tower. "She saw my fire from clear over there."

"You bet she did." Corey called his office, and his secretary, Billie Sanderson, answered.

"I was just leaving," she said. "I waited when I heard you call the tower."

"I want you to phone Sam Harrigan. See if he has a missing-boy report. If he doesn't have it, ask him to check with Thunder Lodge and the other camps."

"Will do, Corey."

"The boy is with me. We'll be down in about an hour."

"Shall I stay to relay Sam's report?"

"No need for that. We're coming right in."

Briss was staring down at the town with a glum look. "That Sam is a cop, huh?"

"Sheriff."

"He's going to put me in jail. I know it."

"No, he's not. All he's going to do is take you back where you belong."

Briss shook his head. "It won't do your old sheriff any good to call Thunder Lodge or Stay-A-Month camp or any other place around here."

Stay-A-Month, eh? The correct name was Stamon's Youth Camp, but the boys who were guests there always called it Stay-A-Month.

Corey was sure now that he had Briss located.

"Don't feel so bad about going back. After you get acquainted, you may like the place. They have some real good counselors there and—"

"Big deal."

Corey took a deep breath. "Want a drink of water, Briss? The Indians used to say that it made their scouts sharp-eyed and alert."

The boy shook his head.

Corey was drinking from the rusty tin can at the spring in the rocks, while Lassie was sniffing at deer tracks in the moss, when the Jeep engine started. Corey shouted as he ran back to the road.

He was too late.

For a hundred yards Lassie ran beside the Jeep, barking a protest. Briss looked very small behind the wheel. The green vehicle gathered speed quickly. Lassie sat down and looked back at Corey.

Briss was driving much too fast on a dangerous road.

THE JEEP was hard to brake because Briss's legs were not long enough to let him put heavy pressure on the pedal. It was the first time he had ever driven a Jeep. Watching Corey handle the vehicle, it had all seemed very simple, but now Briss knew he was in trouble.

Trees and rocks flashed past. On sharp turns the Jeep bounced to the edge of the road. Briss turned off the ignition, but it did not seem to help.

And then he saw ahead of him a hairpin turn where the road doubled back on itself. He knew he could never make it. In desperation he veered into the bank. Dirt had spilled down from the high-cut bank. It made a softness that slowed the Jeep a little.

Then Briss got into the dirt too far and the

sturdy vehicle tilted crazily on two wheels. It almost turned over. He wrenched the steering wheel around with all his strength.

As the Jeep began to skid sideways, Briss looked across his shoulder and saw that the impossible curve was looming closer. He was sure it was all over.

Still, he did not quit. He slid down in the seat and, with one foot on top of the other, pushed the brake as hard as he could.

When the Jeep stopped, Briss was too shaken and scared to move for a few moments. Then he peered over the side. Both back wheels were off the road. He saw great rocks and the tops of trees far below him.

He got out and blocked the front wheels with stones. If he could just get the Jeep back on the road, he would not try to run away with it again. He would wait and take his medicine.

The back wheels dug in and the Jeep settled lower when he tried to move it. Only the rocks he had chocked behind the front wheels kept it from sliding backward. He shut off the engine and got out.

It seemed to him that everything he did went wrong.

After a while he saw Lassie running toward him. She came up to him and nudged against him. For an instant he almost forgot his fear of her. He wanted to put his arms around her and lean against her soft fur, but he did not.

Corey came trotting down the road not long afterward. When he saw Briss an expression of great relief came to his face. But a moment later Briss could tell that the ranger was as mad as he could be.

The boy faced him squarely. He was scared, but he was ready to take what was coming.

"I ought to—" Corey said, but he did not finish. He studied Briss for a few moments, and then he walked past him to look under the Jeep.

Briss wanted to say he was sorry. He really was sorry, and he tried to say so, but nothing came from his dry mouth.

After a while Corey said, "I think I can get it back on the road." He looked at the rocks behind the front wheels. "That was the right thing to do."

"I tried to get it out."

Corey nodded. "Yes, I can see the marks. The trouble was, you had it in two-wheel drive. You're lucky you didn't tip it over backward down the mountain. Now, you use one of those rocks to chock behind the front wheel if she starts to go, and I'll see if I can pull it out."

It made a big difference when the front wheels were pulling. They dug ruts in the road as they inched forward, and the back wheels hurled small rocks far down into the trees.

Then, with a lurch and a bounce, the Jeep was back on the road. Lassie promptly jumped up onto the backseat.

Briss had nothing more to say during the rest of the drive to the valley. He looked wistfully at the boats on the lake as they passed the big blue and white marina west of town.

Corey observed that the four Forest Service

campgrounds on the shore were more than full. You just could not build them fast enough to keep up with the demand, he thought to himself.

The wide main street of Big Sunset was crowded with automobiles. Tourists, campers, and people who had summer cabins in the area thronged the sidewalks.

Corey drove straight to the county courthouse.

Briss swallowed slowly as he looked at the old stone building. He was quite sure there was a jail inside.

Sheriff Sam Harrigan was a tall, lean man with a trim gray moustache and sharp blue eyes.

"Well, well," he said, looking at Briss. "You look like a pretty ferocious customer, son. What's your name?"

"Briss." The boy glanced at Corey.

"Short for Bristlecone Pine," Corey explained.

The sheriff's brows shot up. "Do tell!" He studied Briss shrewdly. "You just go in my office there, Briss, and make yourself at home."

When the door to the office was closed, the

sheriff shook his head at Corey. "We've got nothing on a missing boy. My deputy is still checking, but nothing so far."

That was a surprise to Corey. "Did you try Stamon's?"

"All the camps. I don't expect to find anything on him around here. Judging from how dirty his clothes are, he's been out for several days. If he was from this area, I would have heard about it before now, you can bet."

Corey nodded. "What will you do with him, Sam?"

"Well. . . ." The sheriff was seldom in a hurry about anything. "First, I'll talk to him. You come back in about half an hour, say."

"What for?"

"You found him, didn't you? Don't you want to know who he is?"

"I wish you luck trying to find out. All right, Sam, half an hour."

Lassie was on the courthouse lawn. She looked inquiringly at Corey as he got into the Jeep, and then she trotted to the door of the building.

"He isn't coming with us, Lassie. Come on!"

Lassie still hung back for a few moments before she got into the Jeep. The district ranger's office was a trim log building on a hill a block from the main street. When Corey stopped in front of it, Lassie began to drag Briss's pack from the Jeep.

"Put it back, Lassie."

At his desk inside, Corey looked at the accumulation of mail and unfinished reports. He sighed. Though Billie Sanderson was a wonderful secretary, Corey never did seem to catch up with his paper work.

There were no regular working hours for rangers. You worked until the job was done, and that was it. His mind kept straying as he went through the pile of papers on his desk. He thought of the boy in the sheriff's office.

Outside, Lassie began to bark in a sharp, disapproving tone, and then she scratched on the screen door. As Corey let her in he heard the loud popping of a motorbike. A youth in a red crash helmet was coming up the hill. Because of the noise they made, Corey thought to himself, motorbikes always seemed to be going about four times as fast as their actual speed.

Lassie retreated from the outer office and crouched behind Corey's desk. If there was one thing she had no use for, it was loud bikes.

The youth spun into the yard a few seconds later and tramped into the outer office. He was a gangling lad with a bright grin. On the front of his red helmet was a large, gold figure "1."

"I'm Marty Jackson, road boss of the Red Devils," he explained, looking at the nameplate on Corey's shirt. "Glad to know you, Ranger Stuart."

"What can I do for you, Mr. Jackson?" Corey asked politely.

The youth grinned. "I can see you're happy already about having a hundred Red Devils in your forest tomorrow."

Oh, boy, Corey thought, but he kept a polite expression. Whether or not he liked trail bikes was not the question. "Tomorrow, you say? When do you figure you'll be getting started?"

"At high noon. Our rally calls for us to go over Gold Cup Pass, down to Paywell, and then out to Highway Twenty-nine. Now, what trails do we use?"

"I'll mark some maps for you," Corey said. "You won't be able to go down to Paywell, though, because that trail has been abandoned for thirty years." He glanced at the clock. He was already ten minutes late at the courthouse. "I'll want to talk to your whole group before you start. Can you arrange that?"

Jackson snapped his fingers. "We're at the city campground, most of us. I'll have them together at nine in the morning to hear your lecture."

"It won't be a lecture, Mr. Jackson."

"Briefing, rundown, okay. By the way, Ranger, that campground could stand a little fixing up."

"The town is considering it."

Jackson went out. Lassie eased to the door to watch him. She retreated quickly when he kicked his bike into loud explosions.

"I feel the same way, Lassie," Corey said.

He was leaving when the phone rang. It was Frank Jarvis, a rancher from the Aspen Ridge area.

"Hey, Corey, some of Bill Englemyre's cows are on my grazing allotment. When you going to chase them off there?" He sounded as if he wanted the job done in the next five minutes, though the allotment was thirty miles from Big Sunset.

"Have you talked to Englemyre about it?"

"Naw! You know him and me don't speak."

"Okay, Frank, I'll see him."

"When? Them cows are eating right now!"

"How long have they been there?"

"A week."

More than time enough for Jarvis to have settled the problem himself, Corey thought. But he said merely, "I'll take care of it as soon as possible."

On the way to the courthouse Corey encountered Red Devils blasting up and down Main Street. Every time one of the bikes came close, Lassie crouched low on the seat and growled.

Briss was sitting on a granite slab at the base

of the war memorial in front of the courthouse. He looked dejected and abandoned. Lassie leaped out and bounded over to him, but he offered her no welcome. She sat down a few feet away from him.

Corey went on inside, where Sheriff Sam gave him a wry smile. "I didn't do very well with your boy. He's twelve years old, he came into town on a truck, he has four dollars and ten cents—and his name is still Bristlecone Pine. That's about all I could find out."

"What do you do now?"

"From a few things I picked up talking to him, I'm sure he's a city boy. I've called several nearby cities. If nothing comes in on him by tomorrow, I'll put it statewide."

"In the meantime what happens to him?" Corey asked.

The sheriff shrugged. "The only place I've got for a runaway boy is the jail."

"No! You can take him home with you."

"I would if my wife wasn't away visiting her

folks, and if I didn't have to go to a meeting in Stringville tonight. He'll be all right here. I'll have the night marshal look in on him now and then."

"Jail is no place for that boy, not even overnight!"

"I agree with that," the sheriff said, "but it's all I can do." He shrugged. "Say, do you know how he got over on the south side of the lake? He hitched a ride up to Thunder Narrows and then he made a driftwood raft and paddled over. He must be quite a boy, Corey."

"How do you know he won't run away again, leaving him alone out there on the lawn?"

Sheriff Sam looked surprised. "I never thought of that!" He went to the window. "No, he's still there."

"I'll take him home with me," Corey said.

The sheriff frowned. "Well, I guess I could let you do that. I suppose it would be better than keeping him in my cold, rickety jail."

Suddenly Corey grinned. "You pulled that one on me rather neatly, didn't you?"

Sheriff Sam laughed. "You did it yourself, Corey, but you know doggone well that the boy will be better off with you than anyone else I can think of, until I find out where he belongs.

"He likes you, Corey. He's not a mean kid. Oh, I know he almost started a bad fire, and picked a beef with Bo Wilson's nephew, and tried to swipe your Jeep and doggone near killed himself, but still—"

"He told you all that?"

"Yes, he did." Sheriff Sam shook his head. "But he wouldn't tell me who he was or where he came from."

"And I thought it was just a simple matter of taking him back to Stamon's camp."

"You may have to be responsible for him for more than one night, Corey. I'll keep checking around, but I've got a hunch that boy comes from a long way off."

Briss was still sitting at the base of the monument when Corey went outside. Lassie was lying down with her nose between her paws, watching him as if she were trying to figure what she could do to cheer him up.

"Come on, you two," Corey said. "Let's go home."

Briss hesitated for a moment, and then he jumped up eagerly and ran to the Jeep. Lassie bounced along beside him. She seemed as happy as Briss to get away from the courthouse.

"You could have slipped away while you were out here alone," Corey said. "How come you didn't?"

"I promised the sheriff not to."

"Hungry?" Corey asked.

"Yes, sir."

And about as dirty as a boy could be, Corey thought. Well, a little honest dirt would come off with soap and water. What Briss needed right now was a good hot meal.

Corey headed for the Big Indian drive-in.

THE RATTLE of dishes woke Briss. For a moment he did not know where he was, and then he opened one eye and saw the early sun on the long window in the log wall across the room. He was in Corey's living quarters, a building behind the district office. After eating, the night before, about all he could remember was taking a shower and then falling into bed.

He raised his head when he heard a soft whine. Lassie was standing in the doorway. When she saw him move, she came over to the bed and began to root at the covers.

Before he thought, Briss reached out and patted her on the head. Then the old fear returned and he jerked his hand back under the covers.

When he had been about two years old, he had

crawled out of his bedroom window one afternoon when he was supposed to be taking a nap. After wandering several blocks down the street, he had seen a big dog in a yard and had run happily over to hug it.

The next thing he had known, he was lying on the grass and the huge dog was standing over him, growling deep in its chest, its lips drawn back over broken, yellow fangs. Then a man had run from the house and yelled. The dog had walked away, and the man had picked up Briss. He was not hurt, but he was so terrified that he could not make a sound.

"You're all right, son," the man had said. "He didn't bite you. He's just old and cranky."

Now, Briss looked at Lassie's soft, brown eyes. She was not old and cranky, he could tell, but he could not forget his fear.

From the doorway Corey said, "I see she woke you up."

"I was awake." Briss sat on the edge of the bed. He had scattered his clothes all over the room when he undressed the night before. Lassie found one of his boots under a chair and brought it to him.

"Leave him alone, Lassie," Corey said.

"What's going to happen to me today?" Briss asked.

"First off, breakfast. It's almost ready now, so get with it."

"I mean—"

"One thing at a time, Briss. Get dressed."

Corey was a pretty good cook, Briss decided after he had eaten six pancakes, three eggs, and two slices of ham, and had drunk two glasses of milk.

"Tell me, Briss, won't your parents be worried sick about not knowing what's happened to you?"

Briss shook his head.

"Why won't they be worried?"

"How can they worry when they don't even—" Briss stopped. He had started to say that they did not know he was gone. Corey kept waiting for him to finish, but Briss changed the subject. "If it takes Sheriff Sam a long time to find out about me, can I stay with you?"

"You want to?"

"Yes!"

"I can't promise you that," Corey said. "I'll have to see what the sheriff has in mind."

"He'll let me stay," Briss said confidently. "What do you have to do to be a ranger?"

Corey poured himself another cup of coffee. "You mean, how do you become a ranger?"

Briss nodded eagerly.

"About five years of college, to start. Are you interested in being with the Forest Service?"

Briss thought a moment. "No."

Perplexed, Corey stared at the boy.

"I just wondered, that's all," Briss said. "You want me to wash the dishes or dry them? I'm pretty good at both."

He was a deft, willing worker, Corey observed. They did the dishes and tidied up the kitchen, and then Briss made his bed neatly. "I see you've had practice," Corey said.

"Summer camps." Briss's tone was distasteful.

Briss and Lassie stayed outside for a while after

Corey went to work on reports in the office. It was not long, however, before the boy came inside and stood before the big wall map of the Sleepy Cat National Forest. He studied it quietly for twenty minutes. "Do you know how to read a map?" Corey asked.

"Pretty well. I've got lots of them at home. How big is your Bristlecone Forest?"

Corey put down his pen and leaned back in his chair. "Not very big, really. It's a wonderful area, but we're just getting started on making a scenic reserve of it."

"How old is your oldest tree?"

"We haven't determined that yet. I'd guess thirty-eight hundred years."

"I know one forty-six hundred years old," Briss said. His face was bright and eager. "That's a thousand years older than any redwood. It was growing before anyone built pyramids."

Briss meant Methuselah, a famous Bristlecone in the ancient Bristlecone Pine Forest in California. Corey said nothing. He let Briss go on talking about the trees, until suddenly the boy observed that he was being studied. He immediately clamped his lips shut and the stubborn look came to his face.

"Is your home in California, Briss?" Corey asked gently. "Los Angeles, maybe?"

Briss looked at the floor.

"You say you've seen those trees several times. They're in the Inyo National Forest out there. I'd guess that you must live somewhere close."

"Guess anything you want to," Briss mumbled. He walked quickly toward the door of the outer office.

Billie Sanderson, Corey's secretary, was just coming in. She was a good-looking young woman, slender, with dark, wavy hair. Briss stared at her a moment and then backed away and returned to the map in Corey's office.

When Corey introduced the woman to Briss, the boy glanced at her quickly and mumbled, "How do, Miss Sanderson?"

The secretary and Corey exchanged looks. Corey said, "Would you take him down to Lee's store and get him some new clothes, Billie?"

"There's nothing wrong with my clothes," Briss said.

"I say there is, and that settles it."

Briss wanted to argue, but after a long look at Corey, he changed his mind. "Will I be back in time to go with you when you talk to the Red Devils?"

"Ah, yes, the Red Devils." Corey looked at Billie. "I'll be at the city campground at nine. Drop Briss off there if you're through shopping by that time."

Lassie was not to be left behind. She scrambled into the backseat of Billie's sedan as soon as the door was opened.

Alone, Corey unfolded maps of the Sleepy Cat and marked the trails designated for use by trail bikes. Then he called the sheriff. "Anything on our wandering boy?"

"So far, nothing from this state that fits."

"Try the Los Angeles area, Sam." Corey explained his idea.

The sheriff grunted. "That will take more time

to check out, but I'll give it a whirl. How you two getting along?"

"All right." Corey paused. "Suppose it takes you a week, say, to get the dope on him. In the meantime—"

"I can turn him over to Welfare, and they'll turn him back to me. Then where do I put him—in jail?"

"Yeah, yeah, I know! Stop twisting my arm, Sam."

"I knew you'd see it my way. So long, Corey."

Promptly at nine o'clock Corey was at the city campground. It was jumping with Red Devils. Their small tents were pitched everywhere, between the tables, close to the grills, and even along the driveway. The trash barrels were overflowing.

In spite of the noise the young people were making, a few sleepers were still in their bags on top of the tables.

Corey found Marty Jackson beside a campfire where several girls were cooking breakfast. "Hiya, great white chief of the forest!" Jackson said. He introduced him to the girls, but so fast that Corey could not understand the names.

"Part of the gang is down at one of the campgrounds on the lake," Jackson explained. "I've sent for them. They ought to be here anytime."

"I can wait," Corey said. He explained how he had marked the maps, and then he went over one of them with Jackson until he was sure the youth understood everything he needed to know about the trail designations.

Not long afterward, fifteen more trail riders came roaring into camp on their bikes. They were led by a long-haired blond girl and a grinning boy in a bright green jacket.

It took some time for Jackson to quiet down the camp, and then he introduced Corey. Before he began his talk, Corey saw Billie Sanderson's car arrive at the campground entrance. Briss and Lassie got out and started into the camp.

"I want to welcome you all to the Sleepy Cat National Forest—" Corey began.

"Man, he doesn't know what he's saying!" the boy in the green jacket shouted.

"Shut up, Road Hog!" Jackson yelled. "Let's have order."

Corey smiled. "I've gone over the maps with your road boss, Mr. Jackson. He knows what trails you can use. The forest belongs to you as much as to anyone else. As long as you respect it, stay on the designated trails, and be careful with your fires, you can all have a good time and—"

"That's the idea, daddy!" Road Hog shouted, and once more Jackson had to tell him to be quiet.

"You may meet one of the pack outfits that are in the general area where you're going," Corey continued. "The horses will be ridden by youngsters from the summer camps around here. Some of those horses won't like the noise of your bikes, so I am asking you to be courteous and do everything possible not to spook them. This may mean shutting off your motors if you happen to meet the horses on a narrow trail. That wouldn't be too much trouble, would it?"

"We can do that," a girl said.

"Fine! That's all I have to say. Have a good time, and come back safely."

The Red Devils applauded as Corey walked over to the spot where Briss was waiting with Lassie. When they started toward the Jeep, the big collie ran ahead and leaped in. She was glad to escape the odor of the trail bikes.

"I see you got outfitted, all except the boots and hat," Corey observed.

"She got me a new hat and some shoes, but they don't fit very good," Briss said. "You don't like those kids, do you?"

"What makes you think so?"

"I can tell. You grin and you make a nice speech, but you still wish they'd go somewhere else, don't you?"

Corey laughed. "Yes, I do. It's not the kids, Briss; it's the bikes. If they start short-cutting, they tear up the country and start erosion. I don't like Jeeps, either, if they go where they don't belong. For example, your father doesn't drive his car across someone's lawn, does he?"

Briss did not answer.

As they were driving away, Lassie looked back at the camp and barked, as if saying, "I'm sure glad to get away from that place!"

"You going to marry Miss Sanderson, Corey?" Briss asked.

Startled, Corey repressed a smile. "I don't think so."

"You aren't going to, huh?"

"I don't think her husband would like that, and he's a great big guy who used to teach judo in the Marines."

"I didn't know she was married. I thought—" Briss was suddenly much happier. He stayed outside with Lassie when they reached the office.

Billie was just putting the telephone down. She made a face. "Jarvis again. He's really burning about those Circle Y cattle on his allotment. He's just leaving to go up there."

Corey nodded. "How did it go with Briss?"

"I didn't get him out of that awful hat or those

boots." Billie shook her head. "That boy is suspicious of women, Corey. I wouldn't be surprised to find out that he has a stepmother he can't get along with."

"To tell the truth, I wouldn't be surprised at anything about him. He's an unusual boy. What makes you think he has a stepmother?"

Billie shrugged. "The way he reacts to women. Maybe it's just a bad hunch. By the way, he paid for his own clothes."

"Oh?"

"He dug out a fifty-dollar bill from somewhere. You know, I haven't even seen one of those since I worked at the bank."

"Did you ask him where he got it?"

Billie smiled. "Oh, yes, I asked him, all right. He told me he hadn't stolen it and that it was none of my business." She paused. "I like that boy, Corey. He was rude, yes, but actually it wasn't any of my business where he got that money. He was just defending himself from any slip that might give away his identity."

Corey looked out the window. Briss was walking around the yard. Lassie had a stick and was urging him to throw it for her. "He's a puzzle, sure enough," Corey said. Sheriff Sam would solve the mystery of young Bristlecone Pine, Corey felt sure, though it might take time.

"Call Letty West and tell her that about ten thousand Red Devils will be blasting up her way this afternoon." Letty was the fire lookout atop the steel tower Corey had pointed out previously.

"How many Red Devils?" Billie asked.

"A hundred, I guess. They just sound like ten thousand. There's nothing Letty can do about them, but at least she'll know what's coming off when she hears them." At that moment Corey saw Briss and Lassie coming toward the office. "I'll go up and try to straighten out the allotment situation before Jarvis and Englemyre start shooting each other."

Billie inclined her head toward Briss, who was now close to the screen door.

"Sure, if he wants to go," Corey said.

ON THE WAY to Aspen Ridge Corey explained that they were following an old stagecoach route that had once run over the Flying Horse Mountains.

"I saw it on your map," Briss said. "Why did you block it at the top of the pass?"

"We had this side rebuilt. We have two camp-grounds up here, you see. Loggers use the road when we have a timber sale in this area. Fishermen, ranchers—a lot of people—use it.

"We blocked it at the top because it's all washed out on the other side. Before it was closed, a lot of people, and not just Jeep drivers, either, tried to drive down to the lakes on the other side. They got in all kinds of trouble."

"Do you have to go after them when they get stuck?"

"The Forest Service doesn't *have* to, no, but someone has to. Quite often we and the sheriff wind up doing the job. We don't have wrecker service for idiots who drive right past warning signs and take a brand-new car down a road where a horse has trouble going, but we are concerned about seeing that the people get out all right."

"Why don't you fine them a thousand dollars for going where they're not supposed to?"

Corey chuckled. "We can fine them, but we'd much rather educate them and have their cooperation."

As the road kept rising steadily, Briss looked back and could see the fir-clad hills across the valley where he had been when Corey found him. It sure was big, rugged country, he thought.

After several miles they reached an area of small ridges with aspen thickets and open, grassy parks. Carbonate Creek and its many beaver ponds were on their left. They passed one Forest Service campground. Every space was occupied. On beyond, they saw more cars and campers near the road.

After going through a gate, which Briss leaped out to open, they began to see cattle. Corey stopped to study them. After the third stop, Briss asked him what he was doing.

"An old cowboy like you ought to know, Briss. I'm reading brands to see if those cows are on their proper allotment. Have you been around cattle much?"

Briss hesitated. "I've seen lots of them."

"Where was that?"

"Oh, lots of places where I've been."

Yeah, lots of places, Corey thought. Briss was not going to make any more slips like talking about the Bristlecone Forest.

"What's an allotment?"

"A grazing area designated by the Forest Service for a stockman to run his cattle or horses or sheep on. He pays a fee per head."

"Why can't cattlemen use the whole forest? You told the Red Devils it belonged to everyone."

Corey stopped to look at a small bunch of Herefords. Two of them were Circle Y steers belonging to Bill Englemyre, and they were on Jarvis's allotment.

"Sure, the forest belongs to all the people, but it still has to be managed wisely. You just can't turn cattle loose everywhere. The grass isn't good enough in some places to stand heavy grazing."

"How can you tell?" Briss asked.

Talk about questions! This boy was full of them. "We have range management people who make careful studies to determine how many head of cattle a certain area can stand."

They went another mile before Briss had a new question. "Are these old cowboys going to shoot each other, like you told Billie?"

"I hope not!" Both Jarvis and Englemyre were hot-tempered men who had quarreled with each other for years before they stopped speaking to one another. Though Corey had been joking when he mentioned shooting to Billie, the more he thought about it, the more he worried.

A few miles beyond Tovar Creek campground, Corey saw Jarvis's white pickup in the middle of the road. Jarvis was leaning against it, looking at a bunch of cattle. Before Corey was out of the Jeep, Jarvis began to talk and wave his arms.

He was a big, gray-haired man with small, pouchy blue eyes. He rolled from side to side in a pigeon-toed walk as he came over to the jeep.

"High time you got up here, Corey! Look over there! Circle Y stuff, every blessed head of 'em!"

"I can't tell from here," Corey said. "But—"

"Well, they are! I walked out there to look."

As Briss got out, he saw more cattle in the trees ahead beside the road. Among them was a huge bull. Lassie saw them, too. She took a few steps toward them, and then she came back to Briss.

"I'm paying plenty for the right to run fifty head up here!" Jarvis was saying. "It's your business to see that that thieving old Englemyre stays on his own allotment, and—"

"Now, you just simmer down, Frank. I'll check the cattle, and I'll talk to Englemyre, and—"

"Stall, stall, that's all I get!"

"I had to see for myself what was going on. You

take it easy, Frank. We'll get things settled."

"My old daddy and me ran cattle up here years before you were born, and we didn't have to pay a cent. Now—" Jarvis stopped suddenly. "Talk to him, huh? Well, there he comes. Speak of the devil!"

A red pickup was coming up the road. It stopped behind the Jeep, and a tall, long-jawed man with a growth of stubbly gray whiskers got out. He came stomping up to Corey. "What's that old pot-gut bellering about now, Corey?"

"Pot-gut!" Jarvis howled. "You tell that broken-down bag of bones—"

"Quiet, both of you!" Corey ordered. He explained the situation to Englemyre, who squinted as he looked across the little meadow at the cattle.

"Tell him if he'd put his glasses on, he could read the brands," Jarvis said. "He's been half-blind for years, and thinks nobody knows it."

"Corey," Englemyre growled, "you tell that loudmouth that I'm going to knock his teeth out in a minute if he—"

"You tell him to help himself!" Jarvis yelled.

Englemyre went back to his pickup. With the engine roaring in low gear, he drove off the road and across the meadow for a closer look at the cattle. He went too far, and the front wheels struck boggy ground. He tried to drive on through by giving the pickup more gas. Then the back wheels dug in and sank—and he was stuck.

Jarvis whooped with laughter. "Look at that! He still don't know the difference between a car and a horse!"

Briss was trying to watch several things at the same time—Jarvis, who was whacking his leg and making fun of Englemyre; Corey, who was trying to quiet Jarvis; Englemyre, who was getting his pickup in deeper by racing the engine; and the bull in the trees up the road.

The bull was not taking kindly to all the racket and shouting. He was pawing the earth. He just might get mad enough to come charging down the road, Briss thought.

Englemyre got out of his pickup. He looked at

the back wheels and shook his head in disgust. "It's all his fault, Corey!" he yelled angrily. "I'm coming over there and knock that mule-bray right down his throat!"

For the first time Jarvis spoke directly to his old enemy. "Come ahead, buzzard-bait!"

Englemyre started back across the meadow. Jarvis went to his pickup and dragged out a rifle. "Give me that!" Corey said, walking toward the rancher.

Jarvis levered a cartridge into the barrel. At the same time he swung the muzzle to cover Corey. "You stay out of this, Ranger. You heard him threaten me!"

"Put that down, Jarvis!"

Englemyre was coming on the run. He was about thirty feet away when he saw the rifle. "So that's the size of it! Two can play at that game, Jarvis." He plowed to a stop, turned, and started back to his pickup.

"That's it!" Jarvis shouted. "Go get your rifle and we'll settle things once and for all." He was still keeping Corey at a distance with the threat of his weapon, and Corey was taking no chances.

Disturbed by all the angry shouting, Lassie was leaning against Briss's legs, whining. The boy was so scared himself that he forgot his fear of dogs for the moment. He leaned down and put both arms around the collie's neck.

Suddenly she jerked away and went rocketing into the meadow. At the same time Briss heard the deep bellow of the enraged bull as the animal charged from the trees and thundered toward Englemyre.

Almost together, Corey and Jarvis shouted, "Look out!"

Englemyre broke into a run when he saw the bull. He would have made it to his pickup, but when he looked over his shoulder at the bull, he stumbled and fell. Scrambling on hands and knees, he got up again, but he had lost too much time.

The bull was closing on him. Jarvis raised his rifle and sighted. Corey leaped at him and knocked the barrel up. "Hold it, Jarvis!"

Lassie was streaking across the rough ground.

She intercepted the charging bull, barking as she ran in front of it. The big red and white Hereford veered from its course and lowered its head. Barking, snarling, Lassie was in and out, leaping toward the animal's nose, then scampering away as it tried to gore her.

She led the bull away from Englemyre, clear across the meadow, and into the trees.

During the excitement Corey had taken the rifle from Jarvis, who did not seem to be aware of the fact. Jarvis shook his head. "Whew! That was a close one, Corey. Ornery as that old goat is, I didn't want to see him tromped by a bull."

Englemyre was coming back now. He took off his hat and ran his sleeve across his forehead. "Fifty years in this business," he said, "and that's the closest I ever came to getting it from a bull." He stopped to look over toward the trees. Lassie had done her job and was trotting back unhurriedly.

"That was my own bull, too," Englemyre said.

"You bet it was," Corey snapped. "And on the wrong allotment, like some of those cows over there, and some steers I saw down the road."

"You tell him, Corey," Jarvis said. "If he—"

"Quiet! I'll do the talking for a while, and you two gunfighters can listen."

Corey was plenty mad, all right. Briss could tell. Subdued now, both Jarvis and Englemyre could grasp that fact, too. They avoided looking at each other. Englemyre got out his glasses and put them on.

"I'm going to forget that you pointed a loaded rifle at me, Jarvis," Corey said. "We'll put that down to an evil temper and bad judgment. What I'm *not* going to forget, Englemyre, is that your cattle are on the wrong allotment."

It looked as if Corey had things under control, Briss thought. He went out into the meadow to meet Lassie. Though he did not remember putting his arms around her when he was scared, somehow he was not nearly as afraid of her as he had been before.

She came trotting up and sat down in front of him. She was panting hard.

"Good girl," Briss said. He patted her quickly on the head.

"For one thing, Englemyre," Corey was saying, "if you developed water holes up there where I showed you, your cattle wouldn't be breaking fences to get down here on the creek."

"Yeah, I know."

"Now I'm going to leave it up to the two of you to work this thing out. It isn't part of my job to move cattle. I'll be back here next week, checking again. Can you two promise me you'll have things straightened out by then?"

Jarvis and Englemyre glanced sheepishly at each other.

"It won't take a week," Englemyre said.

"Good!" Corey unloaded the rifle and gave it back to Jarvis. "I think I can pull the pickup out of there with the Jeep, if you tie on in front of me, Jarvis."

Jarvis nodded. He put the weapon in his pickup, as if anxious to get it out of sight as soon as possible.

With the two vehicles pulling, they got Englemyre's truck out of the boggy place. Afterward, Briss stood looking at the deep ruts in the black earth. Down here where the ground was not pitched steeply, those marks would heal over in time, he guessed, but if they were cut into the side of a hill. . . . He could understand better now why Corey did not want Jeeps and trail bikes running cross-country through the forest.

Before Corey and Briss drove away, Englemyre gave Lassie a couple of friendly, grateful pats. "The first time I see you in Big Sunset, Lassie, I'll buy you the biggest steak in town!"

Going back down the road, Briss kept thinking about the whole series of incidents. Some of them seemed sort of funny now, but at the time there had not been anything to make him laugh. "Do you think Mr. Jarvis really would have shot you?" he asked.

"You noticed that I didn't try to take that loaded rifle away from him while he was raving mad, didn't you?"

Billie Sanderson's voice came over the radio. She

was telling Letty at the fire lookout about the Red Devils.

"You know, Briss," Corey said thoughtfully, "maybe I'm begging trouble, but I've got a hunch those Red Devils are going to give us some grief."

Us, Briss thought. That sounded pretty good. He was part of things. He wondered how long it would take Sheriff Sam to find out the truth about him.

AFTER THEY CAME down into the valley again, Corey drove slowly through the Squaw Creek campground on the shore of the lake. Like all the other campgrounds Briss had seen in the Sleepy Cat Forest, this one was overflowing with people. "You ought to build a lot more places like this," Briss observed.

"We try to keep up with the demand," Corey said, "but there are lots of problems involved, the right sites, money, engineering, time—a whole bunch of problems."

He stopped where two young men were emptying garbage cans into a truck. "Hey, Tom, are you ahead of time or late?" Corey asked.

Tom grinned as he came over to the Jeep. "We're late. The truck broke down last night

and we had to go back to Thunder Point campground twice, besides. I had a little argument
with some of those Red Devils up there. They were
scattering soft drink cans all over the place. That
one with purple ostrich feathers on his helmet got
smart, and I had to cool him down."

"Purple ostrich feathers?" Corey said curiously.

"Road Hog, they called him," Briss said. "He
was the one who was yelling while you were
talking, Corey."

"I guess his fluorescent green jacket must have
blinded me. I didn't notice his purple plumes."
Corey glanced toward the Flying Horse Mountains, where the Red Devils had gone.

A man with an ax on his shoulder came over to
the Jeep. "Are you the ranger around here?" he
asked. When Corey said he was, the man complained, "We're out of slabs. A bunch of Kansas
people had a big bonfire last night and burned up
the whole pile. It looks to me like you rangers
could sort of control things a little, so—"

"I'll have some more sent down right away."

"It doesn't bother those people with gas stoves and stuff like that, but some of us use firewood to cook, and—"

"Yes, sir. I'll have some delivered right away."

"If you rangers would come around these camp-grounds once in a while, instead of sitting in your office all day, you'd have some idea of what goes on. There was a fellow with a guitar last night, singing rocky-rolly songs until way after ten o'clock. He kept me awake and then—"

"You'll get the slabs within an hour," Corey said.

As Corey drove away, Briss looked back and saw the man with the ax complaining to Tom about something. Tom was nodding and backing up to resume his work with the garbage cans.

"That old guy was sure a griper," Briss said.

Corey laughed. "We don't get too many like him. He did have a point, though, about those slabs."

Bo Wilson's sawmill was on level benchland about a half mile from the lakeshore. It was a place of buzzing activity. Piles of bright new lumber were stacked for hundreds of feet back from the tin-covered shed where a big saw was whirring through logs to make more lumber.

From another building Briss heard the high-pitched whine of a planing mill. Cabin logs, faced smooth and shiny from the keen knives of another machine, were emerging from a long, tunnel-like shed where four men were working.

What Briss saw mainly, however, was Chub Wilson stacking slabs in a truck after they came off a conveyor near the big saw. The red-headed boy saw Briss, too. They stared at each other and said nothing.

After Corey walked away to find Bo Wilson, Briss got out and stood watching the saw. It was fascinating to see how easily the spinning blade ate through a huge log. The sawyer was a skinny little man who moved briskly without any loss of time in every move he made.

Briss did not hear Chub or see him, until the boy came up from behind and stood beside him.

"Hi," Chub said, speaking loudly because of the noise of the saw.

"Hi."

They looked each other over cautiously. Lassie came trotting over, and Chub petted her. "She sure took up with you, didn't she?"

"I guess she did."

For a while they watched a long log on the carriage as it slid smoothly through the saw.

"You ever been around a sawmill very much?" Chub asked.

"No."

"I can show you how things work. You want to go around with me?"

"Sure."

From over in the stackyard, Bo Wilson and Corey watched the two boys. Chub was pointing and motioning with his hands, explaining the operation of the planing mill.

"Look at them," Bo said. "They're getting along fine. Would you and me be doing that, if we'd just had a knockdown fight?"

"If I'd had a knockdown fight with you," Corey said, "I wouldn't be doing anything now but groaning and looking at the nurse."

"You're tough enough. Don't try to kid me." Bo frowned. "That's what worries me about Chub. He's getting too tough for his own good, being around the mill and in the woods all summer. I don't have any Harvard men working for me, if you get what I mean. I'd sort of like to have that boy grow up halfway civilized, instead of like me."

"Oh, I think he'll turn out all right. Now, about that load of slabs—"

"We'll get them. You'll have to drive the truck down yourself because I can't spare a man right now." Bo paused. "I've been wondering, if Chub had a friend he could run around with—you know, get away from this business and do some of the things normal kids do in the summer—it just might give him a different idea about life."

Corey nodded. "I see what you mean, but you can't pick a friend for a boy—or anyone else."

"Look at them. They're doing fine."

"What are you trying to suggest?" Corey asked.

"That we throw these two kids together. I think it might help Chub a whole lot. They can come up to the cutting area, say, and then you can sort of take them around when you go out. You get the idea?"

"I understand, all right. The trouble is, Briss won't be around very long."

"How long? I had the idea he was going to stay with you all summer," Bo said. "He's a relative, ain't he?"

"No." Corey explained about Briss.

"Oh, I see! You think the sheriff will have him pegged pretty quick, huh?"

"I can't say exactly, but I don't think it will take him too long."

Bo sighed. "Well, I had a good idea, anyway." He pointed. "Take that green truck there. Tell Chub and he'll get a man to load it for you."

Chub and Briss helped pile dry slabs on the truck. Corey studied the boys as they worked. They seemed to be getting along very well. After a time he said, "That's plenty, boys. You want to come along with us, Chub?"

"Yeah, why don't you?" Briss said.

"I'll ask Bo and see if—"

"I already talked to him," Corey said. "Let's go."

The man who had complained about the lack of wood was waiting when they reached the campground. "Huh! That's not much wood you got there."

"The regular crew that services campgrounds will be here this afternoon," Corey said. "They'll see that the place is supplied. In the meantime this should be enough."

"Suppose that guitar player starts in again tonight—"

"Then you'll have to speak to him. Have a good time, sir, and enjoy your stay here," Corey said with a smile.

"Huh! A good time, you say, with no wood, and guitar players all over the place." Almost in the same breath the man said, "That's a fine-looking dog you got there."

Corey saw Briss and Chub grinning at each other. They were laughing as Corey drove out of the campground.

When they returned to the sawmill and Corey started to get into the Jeep, Briss hung back. "Can I stay here with Chub this afternoon?"

Corey looked at his watch. "You haven't had any lunch."

"I've got plenty," Chub said. "I always have plenty."

"I can believe that." Corey thought it over. "What do you fellows figure on doing all afternoon?"

Chub waved one hand. "Just goof around. I didn't have much chance to show Briss the mill. There's a lot of things we can do, Corey."

"All right, as long as you do them here at the mill, so I'll know where Briss is. Okay?"

"Yes, sir," Briss said, and Chub nodded vigorously.

"I'll come by at four-thirty to pick you up."

"I can walk!" Briss protested. "I'll be home then."

Home. It struck something deep inside Corey. Briss had been with him one night, and now he was calling it home.

For a few moments Lassie could not make up her mind when Corey started the engine. She got in the Jeep and then she leaped out. Then she started to get in again, but when she saw Briss and Chub walking away toward the sawdust burner, she barked and ran after them.

Corey ate his lunch downtown. Afterward, he called the sheriff and told him where he had left Briss, and asked if the sheriff had found out anything about the boy.

"Give me time, for heaven's sake! These things don't get worked out in an hour or two, you know."

"All right, all right, Sam! I just thought I'd let you know what I'd done."

"Don't worry about it one bit. I'll take the re-

sponsibility. He'll be all right with young Chub,
you bet."

As Chub had said, he had an enormous lunch.
But he was also a very hearty eater. The two boys
sat on a pile of railroad ties and ate their meal.
Afterward, Briss was still hungry. "I could stand
a malted milk, I think."

"I'm ready." Chub leaped off the tie pile.

They walked down to the highway and found
a hamburger stand, where they both ordered malted
milks and burgers with all the trimmings. While
they were waiting, Chub eyed four boys in Thunder Lodge jackets who were eating at one of the
tables under an awning.

"Summer camp jerks," he scoffed. "Shall we
start a fight with them?"

Startled, Briss asked, "What for?"

"Just for fun. I don't like those summer camp
people."

"Why not?"

"They think they're smart. They run around in

those crummy jackets, and they ride jet boats on the lake—"

"That's not much of a reason for starting a fight, is it?"

"I don't know. It always seemed good enough." Chub grinned. "That Bo, though—boy, you ought to hear how I catch it when he finds out I've been fighting!"

"Does he punish you?"

"Give me a licking, you mean? Naw! But he sure stomps around and bellers. Do your folks give you lickings for starting fights?"

"No. I don't start very many." Briss did not want to talk about his parents. He was glad when he saw their order coming, for he was sure that food would make Chub forget all other matters.

It did, too. Chub did not even pay any attention to the Thunder Lodge boys when they finished eating and walked on toward Big Sunset.

Briss and Chub spent the rest of the afternoon at the sawmill. They sat on a bulldozer, and Chub showed Briss how to operate all the controls, though he explained that his uncle had forbidden him to start the engine.

"I could run this one just as good as the little one up in the woods," Chub said, "but Bo doesn't want me to."

"When are you going back up there to cut trees?"

"Next week. We've got a big rush order for lumber, and that's why the whole crew is down here at the mill."

Heavy machinery had always fascinated Briss. "Do you suppose I could run the dozer up there in the woods, just a little?"

"Sure! I can show you how, and Bo wouldn't mind, if we took it real easy." Chub climbed down. "Come on, I'll show you the big fork."

The big fork was a tall machine on wheels that could be run astraddle a whole pile of lumber. It could pick up the entire stack and load it on a truck. Sitting high in the air, Briss marveled at the rig.

From there, Chub took him into the cab of a huge truck. "This will pull ten tons just like nothing," the redhead boasted. "I know all the gears, but Bo won't let me drive it—except once for a little ways on a straight road."

Before Briss realized it, the afternoon was gone, and it was time for him to get back to the ranger station.

"Come back tomorrow," Bo Wilson told him. "Maybe you and Chub will want to go down to the lake and look at the boats."

"Yeah, we can find a lot of things to do," Chub said.

"I'll see if I can. I'd like to."

"You tell Corey if he don't let you come back, I'll be up there to mop up the place with him." Bo Wilson winked.

The big logger was just about the toughest-looking man Briss had ever known, and in some ways Chub was very much like him, but Briss knew that he liked them both.

He trotted most of the way back to town. Lassie liked that, and tried to get him to go even faster. When he went into the office, he looked at the clock and saw that he was only five minutes late.

"How'd you get along with Chub Wilson?" Billie asked.

"All right, I guess." Briss looked into Corey's office. Bill Englemyre was there, and he and Corey were talking about an agreement with the Forest Service for Englemyre to get material for a new fence on his Aspen Ridge allotment.

"They'll be there another half hour, at least," Billie explained. "Are you in a hurry to talk to Corey?"

Briss was in a hurry, all right. He wanted to ask if he could go back to the sawmill in the morning, and he was wondering, too, if Sheriff Sam had found out anything about him. Sheriff Sam was pretty smart.

He would have to be, if he was going to find out the truth. Briss looked at the calendar. With good luck, he had six weeks. After that, if the sheriff did not find out first, of course, Briss would tell the truth about himself.

"There's something you can do while you're waiting," Billie said. "You'll find a big sack of dog food in Corey's kitchen, and there's a pan just outside the door for water. I think Lassie wants her dinner."

Sitting on the porch outside, Lassie barked agreement. She ran ahead of Briss when he went to the living quarters. He had never fed a dog before. Lassie knew the routine well enough. She sat down before the door where the sack of dog food was stored while Briss was opening the wrong cabinet doors in search of it.

Her whine said, "Here it is! Right in there."

Briss filled a pan with the food and took it outside. Then he filled her water pan and stood well back while she ate. When a dog was eating it might be pretty mean, he guessed.

After he went to bed that night, Briss tried to remember everything that had happened during the day, but it was all sort of a blur. He did know that it had been a wonderful day, however. Tomorrow he was going back to the sawmill, for Corey had promised him that he could.

He fell asleep quickly. Sometime during the

night he thought he heard voices in the living room, but he went right back to sleep and did not worry about the sound.

He had intended to rise very early, so he would be ready to spend the day with Chub, but Corey was up before him, talking to someone in the kitchen. Briss's heart fell when he heard that the visitor was Sheriff Sam.

There could be only one answer—the sheriff had found out everything.

Briss was quite sure of that when he heard the sheriff say, "These deals are always tough to handle, Corey, but at least we got a prompt report on this one."

Briss went on into the kitchen, where the two men were drinking coffee. Now that they had found out, he was ready to face it.

I've rustled up four volunteers," Sheriff Sam was saying. "I don't know how good two of them will be. Five of the kids are ready to go back. With you directing things, that should be enough."

"Plenty," Corey said. He turned to look at Briss. "Good morning, Mr. Bristlecone."

Lassie came over to greet Briss. He patted her neck as he stood there, uncertain now about what was going on.

"Cat got your tongue, son?" the sheriff asked.

"No, sir. Good morning."

"We've got a little problem with two of those Red Devils," Corey explained. "They started down to Paywell from the top yesterday, and they're not there yet."

"I'd give them another two hours," the sheriff

said. "It'll probably be that long before everybody is ready, anyway."

Corey nodded. "I'll keep checking by radio with Stillman. If they come out, they'll have to pass right close to where his crew is working on the gullies below Paywell." He shook his head. "What worries me is what Jackson said last night."

Briss had heard more than enough to know that the sheriff had not come here after him. He breathed a sigh of relief.

". . . so crazy about their bikes, they wouldn't leave them and walk out," Corey was saying. "There're some parts of that abandoned trail where I won't ride a horse. If they slid over one of those cliffs—"

"I doubt that anything that bad happened." Sheriff Sam rose. "I'll have my bunch over here in two hours. Maybe by that time we won't even have to go."

While he was cooking breakfast for Briss, Corey explained what had happened. According to Marty Jackson, the Red Devils had gone to the top of the range. Then, disregarding Corey's orders and Jackson's argument, the Road Hog and a girl named Sandy Hamilton had decided to go on down to Paywell.

After the Red Devils returned to Big Sunset, just before nightfall, they sent a car with a trailer on a seventy-mile trip around the mountains to pick up the Road Hog and Sandy on Highway 29, only ten miles from Paywell.

At midnight the driver called by telephone and said the pair had not shown up, and that was when Jackson came up to the ranger headquarters and woke Corey.

"The fellow on the other side called again about an hour ago," Corey said. "Still no sign of them."

While Briss was eating, Corey went to the office and radioed Bert Stillman, who was in charge of the erosion control project near Paywell.

"We'll keep an eye out for them," Stillman said. "I'll call back if anything turns up."

"If you don't see them by the time you get on the job, send a man up the trail with a radio. Tell him to keep going until we meet him from this side."

Corey took care of several other details. Then he hitched his horse trailer to the Jeep and went down to the Forest Service pasture and got Captain, a wiry, surefooted roan.

When he returned, he found Briss in the office, studying the wall map. The boy's packsack was lying on a chair.

"Where are *you* going?" Corey asked.

"With you, I thought." Briss hesitated. "Can I? I've got a big lunch packed for both of us. I did the dishes and cleaned up and—"

"It's two tough miles to the top of the mountain from where I have to leave the trailer. I've got one horse."

"I don't mind walking," Briss said eagerly.

It was in Corey's mind to say no, flatly and finally, but at the last instant he changed his mind. "All right. You can go as far as the end of the road. From there it's only a short walk over to the fire tower. That's where I want you to stay."

"I won't be helping any doing that." Briss was crestfallen.

"It's that or else you stay here with Billie."

Briss knew better than to argue about it. "Can Chub go, too?"

"If Bo will let him."

"Thanks, Corey!" Briss ran to the phone. From the short time it took him to get in touch with Chub, Corey knew that Chub had been waiting. "It's all right, Chub! We can go as far as the fire tower. Take plenty of lunch."

Two of the sheriff's volunteers arrived with a heavy four-wheel-drive truck and a trailer with two horses. The other two came in a Jeep. Briss blinked when he saw that the driver was the man who had complained about everything in the campground the day before.

"I guess you remember me," he told Corey. "Name's Jake Doty, and this here's my friend, Fred Payne. We heard about them young Red Demons that got lost, so we thought we'd give a hand."

Corey sized them up. They were not young, by

any means, but they were both lean, sun-tanned men. "Glad to have your help," he said. "I hope you know the road only goes—"

"We've been up there," Doty said. "A little walking won't bother us any."

Five Red Devils, led by Marty Jackson, came sweeping into the yard. Before they killed their motors, all the horses were kicking and trying to rear up in the trailers, while Lassie was crowded in between Briss and Chub, growling.

Corey explained the first part of the search plan briefly. The trail bikes were to go on ahead and wait at the top of the mountain for the horsemen and the two men on foot.

At the last moment before leaving, he checked by radio with the fire tower and with Stillman, who had already sent one man up the mountain on the Paywell side. There was still no sign of the two missing people.

Briss and Chub and Lassie rode with Corey to the end of the road. From there, the fire tower, its steel frame shining in the sun, was only a short distance by trail up to a rocky point.

Doty and Payne got out of their Jeep, slung packs on their shoulders, and were gone toward the summit almost before the tail gates of the horse trailers were lowered. Corey watched them go. "Anybody want to bet they don't beat us to the top?"

"No deal with me," one of the searchers said. "I've seen those old coots around all summer. They're like a pair of mountain goats." He put a radio packset on the hood of his pickup and called the sheriff's office.

Corey had another packset, though it was on the Forest Service wavelength. He checked in with Billie, who informed him there was still no word on the missing bike riders.

After looking at the sky, Corey called Letty at the fire tower. "What does your barometer say?"

"It's dropping. I hope we get two inches of rain."

Corey grinned. "Yeah, you up there in your gas-heated penthouse, and us out here in wet saddles. Try to hold that two inches of rain off until tomorrow, will you?" He glanced at Chub and Briss.

"The two boys will be up in a few minutes."

When he was saddled and ready to leave, Corey pointed toward the tower. "Okay, boys. I'll pick you up when I come down."

Briss and Chub watched the horsemen ride away. Lassie whined. Corey had told her to stay with the boys, but she kept looking up the mountain, wanting to follow the horses.

"Is it time to eat yet?" Chub asked.

"No! I don't think it's even nine o'clock."

"I got up early. Maybe I can hold off awhile, though."

Followed by Lassie, the boys went up the trail toward the lookout tower.

A cold wind was blowing across the top of the mountain when the horsemen got there. Jackson and the other Red Devils were huddled behind a big rock. They looked chilled and miserable. Doty and Payne were standing on the very spine of the mountain, studying the country toward Paywell with binoculars.

With one eye on gathering rain clouds, Corey gathered everyone around him and made plans for the search.

"How far down did you last see them?" he asked Jackson.

"It really wasn't far, maybe a quarter mile. The trail bends, and then you can't see it anymore. We heard the motors, though, for quite a while, off and on."

"How were they fixed for spending the night?"

Jackson shook his head. "Not very good—just ordinary clothes. None of us figured on staying up here."

Corey looked at the high point of the mountain, a great mass of jagged rock off to the left. Clouds were already touching it. Below it on the Paywell side, a great sloping basin swooped down from the slide-rock toward the first of the trees at timberline. The Z-shaped scars of old mining trails led up from the grassy basin.

Doty seemed to know what he was thinking. "They couldn't have made it that way, Ranger.

We looked at those trails with glasses, and they're mostly slid in with rocks."

"They never went that way, in the first place," one of the Red Devils said.

"Tracks lead over that way," Payne said.

"Yeah, we went in all directions along the top here, just exploring," Jackson said. "A few even went down the trail to the first bad place and then came back."

"What's Road Hog's real name?" Doty asked.

"George Sharp," Jackson said. "Why?"

"Because I don't want to be looking for somebody called Road Hog, that's why! You fellows shouldn't be allowed in a National Forest to begin with, and—"

"Never mind, Mr. Doty," Corey said sharply. "We're not here to argue about anything." He went to his horse and called Stillman's searcher.

"I'm about halfway up now," the man replied. "I'm working out from both sides of the old trail, in case they had to swing away from it to get around fallen timber."

"We're starting down now," Corey said.

It did not take long to get down into the timber. On the higher reaches of the trail, the marks of the bikes were plain enough. Sandy and the Road Hog had ridden where they could, but at several bad places they had either wheeled or carried their bikes over slide-rock.

Corey and the other riders led their horses at those places, and one man almost lost his mount when it stumbled at the edge of a hundred-foot cliff.

As Corey had expected, the real trouble began in the timber. Fallen trees blocked the old trail in many places. It was tedious work to make detours. The marks showed that the missing young people had experienced great difficulty, also.

Sometimes they worked their way out in one direction, only to find tangled timber that forced them to come back to the trail and go to the other side.

A cold, thin rain began to fall. Fog streamed in across the top of the mountains, hiding them from view a few hundred feet above timberline.

In the heavy timber the searchers continued to shout, but there was no response. Doty and Payne approached Corey. "They never came this far," Doty said. "For the last hundred yards there's no sign of anything going through here but deer and elk."

Soon afterward, they met Arnie Englert, the man who had come up from Paywell. "I never found a track," he said.

Standing under the trees, with the rain drizzling through the branches, the searchers looked at each other quietly.

"We'll go back," Corey said. "Let's fan out as wide as we can and search from here to the top again."

"They should have heard us yelling," Jackson said.

Doty nodded. "Yes, if they were alive."

Jackson started to flare up angrily. "What makes you think they aren't?"

"I didn't say that! What I meant was—"

"All right, calm down," Corey said.

Letty called from the fire lookout just then. "Did you tell the boys they could go home?"

"No. They were supposed to stay at the tower."

"They've been gone for about two hours."

"Maybe they're just hiking around."

"I don't think so. Not in this rain. I can see the turnaround, and they're not sitting in the Jeep. About two hours ago I heard some bikes go up the trail. I'm—"

"Don't worry," Corey said. "They can take care of themselves pretty well." He turned to Jackson. "Were any more of your bunch due to come up?"

"Two more, yeah. They were having trouble with their bikes, but if they got them fixed, they were coming."

The search party went back up the mountain. The Red Devils scrambled along at the base of the cliffs. The heavy fog cut visibility to about one hundred feet, and the rain-slick rocks made the going very slow for the horses on the trail.

At one of the bad places, where the trail sloped

dangerously toward a cliff, Corey and the other horsemen met the two late-arriving Red Devils, who had left their bikes on top.

After everyone had led his horse across the slide-rock, Corey conferred with the late arrivals. "Did you see anything of two boys while you were coming up?"

"We met them down there where the Jeeps were. Two kids with a big collie. The fat one asked us if we could take them up the mountain, so we did. We left them on top."

Corey was more relieved than he cared to show. He would have a word or two to say to Chub and Briss, however, when he saw them.

When the searchers reached the crest, Chub and Briss were not there. Shouts into the ghostly fog drifting across the wet rocks brought no reply.

"How long ago did you leave them here?" Corey asked.

One of the pair who had hauled the boys up the trail looked at his watch. "Almost two hours ago." He pointed east. "We went looking over that way for quite a while before we gave up and went down to meet you guys."

Two hours. Corey had an uneasy feeling. Chub and Briss could have returned to the tower in less than an hour, even without hurrying on the steep trail.

But even before he called Letty, he knew they were not with her, for she would have let him know. "No," she answered. "They're not here, Corey."

"Are both Jeeps and the truck still at the turn-around?"

"Yes."

Corey closed the microphone and looked out at the cold fog. He tried not to show his worry, but it was heavy inside him. Now there were four people lost in the rain and gloomy mists of the thirteen-thousand-foot mountain.

It was chub's idea to ride up the mountain with the two Red Devils. Though Briss had wanted to stay longer in the lookout tower and learn more about it, Chub had grown tired of the cramped space. Lassie, too, was restless, waiting at the bottom of the ladder.

"Let's go explore around," Chub said.

"Don't explore too far," Letty West warned. "It's going to rain before long."

Briss rather liked Letty, mostly because she knew exactly what she was doing in the fire lookout and could explain everything without any stumbling. She was a small, dark-eyed young woman, with a slow, easy way of speaking. She was a senior in college, she told him, and this was her fourth summer in the tower.

"We won't go very far," Briss promised.

He and Chub scrambled down the ladder. Lassie was glad to see them. She was as ready as they were to burn up some energy.

For all his weight, Chub was a good climber. The two boys had a wonderful time scaling the rocky point where the tower stood. Chub said there was supposed to be a bear's den somewhere in the trees below, so they went looking for it. They did not find the den, which made Briss just as happy, but they did discover a spring where deer tracks were thick.

They had lost all track of time when they heard the bikes coming. They ran over to the end of the road, thinking at first that the searchers were coming back from the top. Instead, it was two Red Devils on their way up.

The bike riders stopped at the turnaround while one of them adjusted his carburetor.

"Hey, why don't you guys ride us to the top?" Chub asked.

"Hey, yourself. You weigh too much."

Chub's request had startled Briss, and he did not think the Red Devils were going to pay any attention to it.

"What are you kids doing here?" one of them asked.

"We're with Corey Stuart," Chub said proudly. "How about taking us up, huh?"

"No, Chub. Corey said—" Briss protested.

"Not a bad idea, Jerry," one rider said to his companion. "She gets real steep from here up, and I've been spinning quite a bit already. What are you guys going to do when you get up there?"

"Come back," Chub said.

"Hop on," Jerry said. "I can use the weight."

Briss held back. "Corey said to stay here."

"Aw, what's the difference? We'll go up and then come right back. Don't you like to ride on a bike?"

Briss guessed that it really would not hurt anything. It was only two miles, and they could come down the trail in no time.

The Red Devils made the run in a short time.

Chub leaped off at the top, grinning. "Boy, that was fun!"

"Okay, you boys had better beat it on back now," Jerry said.

Briss was of the same opinion.

"Where you guys going now?" Chub asked.

"We're going to scout around over that way. We were all over the top yesterday. About a mile east the Road Hog saw a place where he thought maybe he could get a bike down."

"But they went down the trail, Jackson said." Briss looked at heavy, gathering clouds.

"They started down, but maybe they came back later and tried somewhere else. Anyway, there's a whole slew of people looking down the trail." Jerry and his companion walked off to the east.

Chub was studying the row of bikes. "I'm going to get me one of those someday." He turned away from them reluctantly. "Well, I guess we'd better get started."

Lassie was sniffing around in the rocks on the left side of the pass. She had stayed quite a distance behind the bikes on the way up, and still did not want to get too close to them.

Now it was Briss who suddenly wanted to do something that Chub was opposed to. "Let's go look over that way, Chub."

"Naw! We'd better get back."

"Just a little ways. Maybe we'll find some tracks."

"Sure, you'll find tracks! You heard Jerry say they went all along the top here. Let's beat it."

"It'll take only a little while." Briss started west along the mountain. Lassie ran to join him, and soon Chub called for them to wait for him.

For a while they found a good deal of evidence that the Red Devils had explored along the ridge— drops of oil on the rocks, marks where a tire had spun, and here and there a candy bar wrapper.

And then they saw no more signs. They were now in an area where huge rock masses towered above them. They had gone around a shoulder of the mountain, and could no longer see back to the place where the bikes were parked.

Chub looked ahead doubtfully at shattered granite running sharply down the mountain. They were on the same side they had come up, forced that way because the north side of the crest was almost sheer.

"This is far enough," Chub said. "Nobody could ever get through that mess with a bike. Let's get out of here."

Briss was about ready to agree. On one of the maps in Corey's office he had seen some mining trails marked on this part of the mountain, but he could see no evidence of them from where he now stood.

Somewhere in the rocks below them Lassie began to bark.

"Probably a coney or something," Chub said. "Come on, Lassie!"

The collie continued to bark until Briss and Chub climbed down to see what had excited her. She was on an old trail, and there were the tire marks of two bikes in it.

Chub's eyes grew big as he looked at Briss. "Maybe—maybe they *did* come this way."

The trail ran on ahead for a short while, then

disappeared into the jungle of tumbled granite. Briss debated whether to follow it or to go back and try to find Corey and the others.

Chub hunched his shoulders and looked around at the bleak rocks uneasily. "It's going to rain."

Lassie went on ahead. After a moment's hesitation the boys followed her. The trail led farther and farther into a wild jumble of stone. In some places the mountain had almost obliterated it, but the two Red Devils had still gone on, carrying their bikes across the bad places.

They passed old prospect holes dug into the red-stained rocks of an iron dike. Now they were a long way from the trail to Paywell. A bitterly cold rain began and fog drifted across the mountain. Suddenly the trail began to go up steeply.

Looking at slide-rock ahead, Briss said, "I think I remember this trail from the map. It goes around the mountain to a mine."

"You and your maps," Chub grumbled. He hunched his shoulders unhappily. "I'm hungry."

"I'm scared," Briss said, "but we've got to go on."

"Maybe they're dead," Chub said gloomily. "Maybe they rolled about a mile down there in the rocks somewhere."

That thought had occurred to Briss. He looked at Lassie, already up on the dangerous slide-rock, waiting for them to go ahead. "Let's go as far as we can, Chub."

"All right, but I don't like it."

Lassie led the way across the slide-rock. Briss scrambled after her quickly. When Chub came across, some of the rock slid under his feet and poured down the mountain. It made a hollow, booming sound somewhere far below.

They found tire marks again. Chub shook his head. "Boy, they'd better quit taking their bikes across places like that!"

In places the trail was as good as when some unknown miner had blasted it from the side of the mountain, but where rocks had slid into it, it was scarcely a trail at all.

They struck a place where a great spill had come from above. For fifty feet there was no trail, though

they could see it on the other side. Lassie went skip-
ping across. Briss hesitated. He knew how loose
those rocks were. "We've got to run," he said.
"That way you keep ahead of where it slides."

Chub was looking below. "There they are!
Look!"

Briss saw the bikes then. They were almost
obscured from vision, down in the slide-rock where
the spill had jammed against enormous slabs of
granite. He was afraid of what else he would see,
but as he kept peering below, he could see only the
bikes lying there in the rain.

Then Lassie barked. She was out of sight somewhere in the fog. The sound was muffled, but there
was no mistaking the urgency of her tone.

"Wait till I get over," Briss said. He ran, with
the rocks moving under his feet at every jump. He
made it to the other side and waited.

With his round face screwed up as if in anger,
Chub made his run. He almost fell once, but he
recovered and charged on till he reached Briss.
They went around two sharp turns.

Looming ghostly in the dim light, a weather-beaten mine building stood against a sheer wall. The door was open. Lassie was jumping around in front of it, barking.

And then the boys heard a girl's voice.

She hobbled into the doorway. Briss recognized her at once; she was the blond girl who had ridden beside Road Hog. She kept looking on beyond the boys. "Where're the others?" she called.

"How do you like that?" Chub muttered. "We find—"

"Easy, Chub," Briss said. "Are you all right?" he called back.

"We're alive, if that's what you mean," Sandy said. "Where're the others?"

It was not much of a building, the boys saw when they went inside, but at least it had sheltered the two. The Road Hog was lying on some boards, with one leg in a splint. His red helmet with the plumes was beside him, the plumes broken and bedraggled.

He did not look very good, Briss thought, but

still the Road Hog grinned. "So they sent a couple
of boys to do a man's job, huh? We're glad to see
you, anyway."

Sandy was using a board as a crutch. "Just you
two?" she asked.

"We'll get somebody else," Chub said. "What's
the matter with your leg, Road Hog?"

"It's broken. Not bad, I hope."

"We slid off that last place, both of us," Sandy
said. "I sort of sprained my ankle, I guess."

"She did that when she was helping me up to
this place," Road Hog explained. "How far behind
are the others?"

"Not far." Briss tried to be cheerful, but he was
scared and scarcely knew what to do. They would
have to go back over that terrible trail and try to
find Corey.

He looked at Lassie. An idea came to him, and
for the first time he had no fear of her. But would
she understand what he wanted?

He went outside with her and pointed down the
trail. "Go find Corey, Lassie," he pleaded. He gave

her a little shove, and then he went with her a short distance along the trail. "Corey, Lassie! Go find him!"

For a while he thought she did not understand. And then the big collie whined and set off down the trail at a run. Briss saw her flash around the first turn. After that she was out of sight.

He looked at the gloomy fog which seemed to be growing thicker every moment. Maybe he should have gone himself, he thought. But Lassie could do it so much faster. Knowing very little about dogs, he was not sure that he had done the right thing.

When he went inside, he found Chub tearing boards off a storeroom to build a shelter over the Road Hog to protect him from the rain dripping through the cracks in the sagging roof.

Sandy was sitting on a box, looking at her swollen ankle. "I'm sorry, Briss, that I seemed disappointed when I first saw you boys. Chub has explained how you happened to find us." She hesitated. "Will the dog know what to do?"

"Lassie? Sure, she will!" Briss hoped so.

Chub finished the shelter over Road Hog, who still had a grin, though he was flushed with fever. "You're a pretty handy guy with your mitts, Chub."

It seemed like a very long wait in the old ruined building. Briss kept going to the door every few minutes to look along the trail. He did not happen to be watching outside, however, when Lassie returned. Her fur was wet and parted down the middle of her back from the rain.

She barked a happy hello as she came dashing in.

Briss and Chub ran to the door. They could see no one on the trail. They looked at each other, both afraid that Lassie had merely gone away and returned, without finding anyone.

Then they heard rocks rattling down the mountain, and the sound of voices. Not long afterward, Corey, with the two old-timers, Doty and Payne, came in sight.

Briss stooped down and hugged Lassie, wet fur and all.

Sheriff sam tossed a newspaper across the desk to Corey. "I thought that might be a big help, but it won't."

Corey had seen the story in a city newspaper the evening before. It gave a great deal of credit to Charles Wilson, Briss Cone, and Lassie for "their heroic efforts in the rescue of two injured people." Several pictures accompanied the story.

Corey smiled. "Look at that grin on Chub."

"Yeah. And look at that blur on Briss's face. You know what? He moved, and he did it deliberately."

"It's a good picture of Lassie."

"That kind of story has a lot of appeal. Two boys and a dog find lost bike riders. The wire service sent that picture all over the country, Corey." The sheriff shook his head. "The trouble is, if Briss was your own son, you wouldn't recognize him. He moved, I tell you."

"Why didn't you tell the reporters he was a runaway, Sam? They would have made a big deal of that."

"Why didn't *you* tell them?" the sheriff asked. When Corey did not answer, Sheriff Sam said, "You kept quiet because you figured I'm pretty close to getting the answer."

"Are you?"

The sheriff gave Corey a sheet of paper. "I took that report yesterday by telephone from Los Angeles."

Corey read the scribbled notes carefully. The description fitted Briss very closely. The name of the missing boy was Robert Joseph Crisman, age twelve. His father was an aircraft engineer, "presently unavailable for interview."

"The time doesn't check," Corey said, frowning. "This says he was reported missing three days ago. Briss was here then."

"I know." The sheriff leaned back in his chair.

"Sometimes when a kid is out of sight for an hour, parents will get frantic and call the police. And then you've got the kind that are afraid of looking bad because their kid ran off. They'll try to find him themselves, calling all the relatives and friends —that sort of thing—before they ever get around to notifying the police."

Corey put the paper down.

"You seem to have some doubts," the sheriff said.

"I just don't know. The description is mighty close."

"It may be even closer when the Los Angeles police give me his medical and dental record. I'll get that by mail, but if there's anything in it that will offer positive identification, they'll call me as soon as they have it."

"Okay, Sam. I'll go up and get him whenever you say." Corey started out.

"I thought Bo Wilson's crew came in every night."

"They do, but he won't be back to cutting until the first of the week. In the meantime I let the boys go up to the Cyclone Peak guard station. They wanted to camp out, but I thought they'd be better off in a cabin."

The Cyclone Peak guard station was a solidly built one-room cabin at the edge of a meadow that held four large beaver ponds. Briss and Chub had found no end of things to do during their stay there. One day they hiked up the Cyclone Trail to the top of the mountains. From there they could see a hundred miles in three directions, and across the valley to the peak where they had found the Road Hog and Sandy.

"It's a good thing some rich guy doesn't own all this country," Briss observed, "or we couldn't even come up here."

"You're getting to sound just like Corey and Bo."

"I guess so." Briss watched Lassie walking slowly along the crest, her head high, her long hair stirring in the wind. He no longer had any fear of her. She made a beautiful sight, he thought, pacing along the rocks against the clear blue sky.

She stopped suddenly and looked hard at a steep wall of rock a half mile away.

"There's something over there," Briss said.

Both boys saw the goats at the same time. They looked at first like two white blotches on a sheer cliff. Unhurriedly the animals moved along the wall where it did not seem possible to find any kind of foothold. Then they went straight up.

"Look at that!" Chub cried.

The goats gained a ledge, and there they stood, looking across the chasm at the two boys and Lassie.

"You know something?" Briss said. "I've read that there's less known about Rocky Mountain goats than any animal in all of North America— and we're looking at two of them."

They watched until the goats moved on up the cliff and out of sight.

"Boy, wasn't that something?" Chub said. "I wonder if they're good eating."

On the way back down the mountain they encountered a colony of marmots, stocky, yellowish animals that Chub called whistle pigs. Lassie went over to investigate them. Sitting high on a rock, one of the whistle pigs much larger than the others made a shrill sound.

Lassie walked slowly toward him. He disappeared into the rocks, and another one popped up behind her and whistled. Lassie whirled around. That one disappeared, and another marmot appeared behind her and made its shrill noise.

As she stalked away in a dignified manner, her attitude plainly said, "I have no more time to fool around with your silly little game."

Chub and Briss looked at each other and laughed. Lassie chose to ignore them, too.

At an old cabin in a flat below, Briss found a purple bottle half-buried in the pine needles. He washed it in a little stream and held it up to the light. "People in California think these old purple bottles are wonderful."

"Tourists around here do, too," Chub said. "They root around in old dumps looking for them.

There's a guy in town who pays kids two bits for every one they find, and then he sells them for about three bucks."

"I'm going to keep this one."

Later, farther down the trail, Chub asked, "That's where you're from, huh—California?"

"How do you know?"

"You just said so, didn't you?" Chub shrugged. "I don't care if you ran away. Bo told me about you, but I didn't tell anyone else, and neither did he. Why *did* you run off?"

"Because I did, that's why."

"Okay, okay, it's your business." Chub threw a rock at a stump. "Only I was thinking— Aw, never mind."

"Never mind what?"

"Nothing!"

"You started to say something," Briss said hotly, "and then you wind up with 'never mind.' That's no way to talk."

"Yeah? Well, running away from home is not so good, either, Briss. Me, I never had any parents.

Sometimes I'm jealous of kids that do. At school they're all the time talking about their mothers and fathers, so I just pretend I like it better not having any." Chub shook his head. "But that isn't so."

Briss was silent. He had assumed that Chub was happy as could be, living with his uncle and having the freedom all summer to work at the mill or go to the woods. He had just seen a new side to Chub.

Briss had little to say the rest of the way to the guard station. He was quiet during dinner. When he went outside to empty the dishwater, he stood for a while looking at the mountains.

He went inside and hung the dishpan on its nail. Chub was lying on his bunk, listening to his transistor radio.

"The guy says the Road Hog is getting along fine at the hospital. Sandy's ankle wasn't busted, just sprained."

"Did he call him Road Hog?" Briss asked.

"Naw! George Sharp."

Briss put a stick of wood in the stove. He walked restlessly around the small room, frowning.

"What's the matter, Briss?"

"If I tell you about myself, will you keep still?"

Chub did not answer hastily. "I won't tell," he said finally.

"You promise?"

"Yes, I promise."

Briss sat down on the edge of one of the bunks. "My parents aren't worrying about me because they're in Europe. They're getting letters from me twice a week from a boys' camp in the Sierras. It'll be about a month before they get back. By that time I guess I'll be home."

Chub put his radio on his stomach. "How are they getting letters from you?"

"I suppose my grandmother is sending them on. I was staying with her, after my dad and Judy left. You see, at this summer camp they make you write home twice a week, so I just wrote all the letters at one time and gave them to Bobby Crisman to mail."

"I get it," Chub said. "This Bobby is at the camp."

"Yeah, in my place. I sent him there."

Chub stared at his friend. "Wow! That's real sneaky." He frowned. "Someone knows that Bobby's missing, don't they?"

Briss looked at Lassie sleeping on an old blanket near the woodbox. "Maybe not. He's supposed to be on a tour with a Boy Scout troop in Canada. They might have found out that he didn't go, by now. I don't know." Briss shrugged.

"Anyway," he went on, "he's always missing. He's run away three times. His father works for the government, some kind of secret deal that keeps him away from home most of the time. Bobby's mother divorced his father, so Bobby stays with his cousins part of the time, and sometimes he stays with his aunt."

Chub shook his head. "I still don't see how you worked it."

"It was easy. Bobby was supposed to leave on the bus tour the day before I was due to go to camp. He had to have a parent or guardian with him at the station to sign some papers. We knew Bobby's aunt would say she was awful busy—she always says that—so we told her the man had said it would be all right for Bobby to come down without her.

"There's this harmless old guy who sits around on benches downtown in Los Angeles. They call him the Colonel. We gave him ten bucks to pretend to be Bobby's father and sign the papers. I guess the old Colonel is some kind of bum, but he sure doesn't look like it. It was easy. The Colonel said Bobby's grandmother had died, and then he signed the paper that canceled the trip for Bobby."

"Boy, that sure is crooked!" Chub cried.

"Wasn't it better for Bobby to go to summer camp than to run away again? That's what he was figuring on. I called him when I was on my way here. He said he was doing fine."

"But his folks don't know where he is!" Chub protested.

"If he'd run away again, they would know even

less. They probably still think he's on the bus tour. He's all right." Briss shook his head.

"Pretty crooked, is all I got to say. I suppose you used the same old bum to sign Bobby off to camp?"

"Yep! Bobby stayed with me and my grandmother that night, so his aunt wouldn't know he was still around. My grandma is pretty old. She doesn't like to go downtown. I told her she didn't have to go to the bus with me, but she was going to go, anyway.

"Then I told her I'd have the summer camp guy in charge of the bus call her after I got to the station, just to prove that everything was all right. She agreed. The old Colonel charged us another five bucks to make the call. Then he signed the papers and away Bobby went—under my name, of course.

"I beat it, too. I caught the first bus headed this way. Then I rode the train for a while. The last fifty miles to Big Sunset, I had to ride on a truck."

"You were going just any old place, huh?" Chub asked.

Briss shook his head slowly. "I was coming to see the Bristlecone Pines."

"What!" Chub was mystified. "Is that all?"

"It isn't just 'all,' Chub. It's kind of hard to explain. My dad took me to the Bristlecone Forest in California several times." Briss knew it *was* hard to explain, even to himself. "Those were about the only times we ever went anywhere together.

"We had a lot of fun. We were going again this summer, for a whole week." Briss paused, shaking his head. "And then my dad said he couldn't make it. He said he had to take my mother to Europe. She isn't my real mother. She's not like my real mother was at all."

"So you got mad and ran off."

"My dad ran away from me, didn't he? Summer camp again for me. It wouldn't be so bad if they weren't sending you there just to get rid of you. Sure, I ran away!"

Chub was silent for a long time. "I won't tell

on you, Briss, but maybe *you* ought to get all those lies straightened out by telling the truth to Sheriff Sam."

"No! I'll go home when my dad comes back. I didn't lie to Sheriff Sam, except for one thing. I said I had only about four dollars, when I really had about seventy."

"What was the idea?" Chub asked.

"Because I knew he would put it in his safe, and then I wouldn't have anything to use to run away. Then he said he'd let me go outside if I promised to stick around. After I promised, I had to stay."

"It's still a pretty crooked thing," Chub said. "But I said I wouldn't tell, so I won't." He turned on his radio and held it to his ear. "Old Sheriff Sam will find out about you, you bet."

"I don't think so."

CHUB WAS AN early riser. He was out of his bunk and making pancakes while Briss was still trying to wake up.

"Get him out of there, Lassie!" Chub said. "We've got lots of things to do today."

Briss reached out to hug Lassie when she began to root at his sleeping bag. He wondered why he had let his fear of dogs last so long.

"The first thing we've got to do," Chub announced, "is to catch some fish. We ate all the hamburger last night, so we've got to have some fish."

"*You* ate it all, you mean." Briss grinned. The serious conversation of the night before was behind them, and he was ready to enjoy the day.

"It's gone, anyway," Chub said.

After breakfast they were careful to leave the cabin orderly before going to the beaver pond. Corey had left two fishing rods and other gear. Within an hour they had ten fat cutthroat trout.

"That's plenty for now," Briss said. "No need to catch any more than we can use."

They cleaned the fish and put them in the screened cooler on the shady outside wall of the cabin.

For the rest of the day they explored the area around the guard station. Chub knew the different trees at a glance, and he was happy to identify them and show his knowledge of their various uses for lumber.

"This is pretty high for Douglas fir," he told Briss, "but there's quite a bit of it around. See how the cones hang down? They've got three snake tongues sticking out between the scales."

Ever since his first visit to the Bristlecone Forest, Briss had been interested in trees. He had read a good deal about them in Forest Service publications, but he did not make a display of what he had learned to Chub. He kept quiet and learned a little more, instead.

"We're cutting Douglas fir on Silver Bear Creek," Chub said. "Boy, it sure makes good lumber. Hey! Bo will have the crew there, starting tomorrow. Did Corey say you could come up?"

"It wasn't settled, but I think he'll let me."

"Anyway, we've got two more days to stay here before Corey comes after us."

They were following a game trail sometime later, when Lassie stopped and began to growl. She got between the boys and an open space ahead, moving in a slow, stiff-legged walk.

"Look! Over there on that bare hill," Briss whispered.

It was the first wild bear he had ever seen. Its reddish-brown coat was gleaming in the afternoon sun as the animal tore at a rotten log.

"He's getting grubs and ants and stuff from that old log," Chub whispered. "Boy, look how strong he is!"

"Mean?" Briss asked.

"Naw! Unless it's a mother bear with cubs. I don't see any cubs around. Let's get closer."

"This is close enough." Lassie seemed to think so, too. She crowded against Chub's legs when he started to leave the timber.

"Well, maybe we'd better not bother him," Chub decided.

They never knew what alarmed the bear. It sat up suddenly and moved its head from side to side. Then, in a rolling, humping run, it went across the hillside and disappeared into the trees.

They went over to see what the bear had been eating. Big black ants were swarming in the rotten wood. Lassie sniffed and growled, and her hair rose. When Briss walked a few steps in the direction the bear had gone, Lassie made him stop.

It was then that Briss saw the cub in a tree. Remembering what Chub had said about mother bears, he pointed, whispering, "Let's get out of here."

"Don't run," Chub cautioned, his voice quavering. "Just walk away easy."

They were trying to do just that, though somehow going faster and faster all the time, when the mother bear came to the edge of the timber. She stood up and watched them.

"D-Don't do anything to make her think we're scared," Chub said.

Suddenly, with a deep grunting roar, the bear charged.

"Run!" Chub yelped.

Briss did not need the advice. He was already running.

Behind them they heard Lassie's barking and the savage grunting of the bear. Chub was still a step or two ahead of Briss when they reached the timber. They glanced back then.

Lassie had led the bear away from them. She was zigzagging along the hill, barking, daring the big bear to chase her. Satisfied that the nimble dog was no great threat, and certainly impossible to catch, the bear went ambling back to her treed cub.

Chub and Briss trotted down the game trail a

long way before they slowed to a walk. Lassie caught up with them. She was panting and wagging her tail. She seemed to be laughing at them. After they praised her for her action, she went trotting down to the creek for a drink.

Though Corey was not supposed to come for them until two days later, his Jeep was at the guard station when they got there. Something had come up, Briss thought, something about him.

"Remember your promise," he told Chub, and Chub nodded.

Corey stepped out of the cabin. "You boys look as if you've been enjoying yourselves. I want to congratulate you on keeping the guard station in good shape."

Excitedly they told him about their experience with the bear. Corey nodded soberly. "It's a good thing you had Lassie with you." He looked at Briss. "I'm taking you boys down right away, so get your things together."

Briss did not ask any questions. He was sure that Sheriff Sam had found out about him. From the look on Chub's face, he knew that Chub was thinking the same thing.

It was late when they reached Big Sunset. Corey drove to the Medical Clinic, a long, brick building on a point overlooking the lake. "You may as well come in, Chub," he said.

Dr. Nye was young, crew-cut, and brisk. After looking Briss over for a few moments, he said, "Have you been hiking in those cowboy boots?"

"Yes, sir." Briss looked down at his boots. "They are getting sort of bad, I guess."

"Bad isn't the word for it. Take your shirt off, and stand right there."

Dr. Nye examined Briss's right arm, digging deep with his fingers. He looked at his teeth. "You're barking up the wrong tree, Corey."

"You're positive?"

Dr. Nye smiled. "I can have X rays taken, if the sheriff insists, but I can assure you that they'll show the arm was never broken, and they'll show teeth in two sockets where the record says there are no teeth."

"Good enough for me," Corey said. "Put your shirt on, Briss."

They did not leave the clinic immediately. Corey took them down the hall to see the Road Hog, who was flat on his back with his leg elevated in a cast.

"Old Smokey Bear, himself, and his two cubs! Nice to see you." The Road Hog grinned.

One thing about the Road Hog, Briss thought, nothing seemed to get him down. They visited with him for a while, though Chub and Briss could not think of much to say.

Then the Road Hog asked Corey, "You'll be at that hearing, won't you?"

"Oh, yes."

"I phoned twenty-five of them myself, from right here. Jackson must have called twice that many. I think we'll have a good representation, Ranger."

Later, in the Jeep outside, Briss asked what hearing the Road Hog had been talking about.

"It's a public hearing about trail bikes in the Sleepy Cat Forest," Corey explained. "Those for and those against, or anyone at all, can attend and state their views." He started the Jeep and drove toward Chub's home. "We try to get specific suggestions from both sides, and then we try to work out the problems to the best advantage of everyone.

"It isn't a simple deal, believe me. Horseback riders can get awful mad when bikes scare their horses off the trail. I can get pretty mad when I see where trail bikes have cut up a slope and started an erosion problem. And bike riders can get howling mad when we tell them trails are closed to them."

"Is that what old Road Hog is getting all the bike riders for—to be howling mad at your meeting?"

Corey laughed. "To tell the truth, the first public hearing we had on trail bikes was just about that way. Everyone was mad. But now I'm sure we're going to get some real cooperation and some good suggestions from the Red Devils, and that's better—"

Corey stopped the Jeep to watch a water skier

skimming along behind a jet boat. The jet was throwing a big rooster tail that was catching the last of the sunset glow.

"Boy, that looks like fun!" Chub said.

"That's a fair example of what I'm trying to say," Corey said. "Mechanical power. It creates problems in the National Forests."

"Don't you like engines and stuff like that?" Chub asked.

"Sure, I do, but I don't want to see the National Forests overrun with mechanical gadgets. First, it was Jeeps, and then trail bikes, and before long there'll be one-man helicopters. How would you like to be fishing a high lake, say, after walking ten miles—and then have some fat, lazy character set down smack in front of you in a helicopter?"

"I'd ask him to let me take a ride in it," Chub said.

Corey chuckled. "I'll bet you would, at that." He drove on. "No, it's not that I'm against modern machines, but you've got to remember that a lot of people go to the mountains just to enjoy quiet and peace. Our problem is how to balance out the many uses of the National Forests so that everyone can use and enjoy them."

Briss had been listening quietly. "That doesn't sound easy to me."

"No, it isn't. That's why I'm pretty happy about the Road Hog's idea of working with us on the matter of trail bikes. He's got the Red Devils working, not only in their club, but with other groups, too, to set up some codes of behavior. I think it's a very good start on a problem that's getting bigger every day."

"Old Road Hog," Chub said. "I guess he learned something when he slid off that trail where he wasn't supposed to go." He hopped out when Corey stopped at his house. "Briss isn't the one you and the sheriff thought, huh?"

Corey shook his head. "Not unless his name is Bobby Crisman. How about that, Briss?"

"That isn't my name."

Chub studied the ground before asking, "Can he go with me to the woods tomorrow?"

"I'll have to check with the sheriff, but I think it'll be all right." Corey smiled. "That is, if you take Lassie along to fend off bears."

Briss grinned. The way he and Chub had run from that mother bear must have been a funny sight, though at the time it had not been very amusing. He was feeling great. Tomorrow he could go to the woods with Chub, and maybe Bo Wilson would let Chub start right away to show him how to run the dozer.

But something was bothering Briss, and it continued to grow as he thought about it. Ever since Chub had said that the trick he and Bobby had pulled at the bus station in Los Angeles was crooked, Briss had been troubled.

If no one was worrying about either of them, maybe it would not be so bad, but now Bobby's folks knew he was missing. Of course, it wasn't the first time Bobby had run away. Briss tried to console himself with the thought that maybe Bobby Crisman's aunt would not get too excited about his being gone.

They had always found him before, sooner or later.

As they drove away from Chub's house Corey asked, "Is something eating on you, Briss?"

"No!" Briss said quickly. *Briss*. He had come to like that name, but suddenly it seemed strange to him. David Brian Russell. That was his real name.

A stubborn streak rose in him when he saw that Corey was driving to the courthouse. While Briss and Lassie waited outside, Corey talked to Sheriff Sam. When the ranger returned, he told Briss the sheriff would like to talk to him for a few minutes.

Briss took Lassie in with him.

"Quite a bear dog you've got there," Sheriff Sam said. "Corey was just telling me about you and Chub."

"Yes, sir."

Sheriff Sam talked all around the subject that Briss knew was on his mind. He did it so easily and naturally that Briss almost made some slips answering questions.

"So you're still not ready to help me, Briss?"

"No, sir, not the way you mean."

Sheriff Sam smiled. "And you still insist that your parents are not worrying about you?"

"You mean if my dad—" Briss caught himself. "No one is worrying."

"That's odd. They must not know you're gone, huh?"

Briss looked at the floor.

"I suppose your stepmother treats you pretty mean?"

"No, sir, she doesn't! I—" The best thing, Briss decided, was to keep his mouth shut.

Sheriff Sam kept studying him quietly. "You're very sure they don't know you're gone?"

Briss did not answer.

"So you're going to the woods with Bo Wilson's crew in the morning?"

"Yes, sir."

"Well, have a good time and be careful." Sheriff Sam's face was sober, but his eyes twinkled as he added, "And watch out for bears."

EVERY DAY FOR a week Briss went to the timber cutting on Silver Bear Creek. He and Chub and Lassie rode with Bo Wilson in one of the huge trucks. Now that Briss and Chub were friends, Bo did not want Chub to help with the work.

The first day they arrived at the cutting, Bo waved his arm and said, "Now, look, why don't you boys take Lassie and hike up to the Signal Hill caves? Maybe you can find one of those Indians supposed to be buried up there."

"Who wants to find an old skeleton?" Chub said. "Briss wants to stick around here, so I can show him how to run the dozer."

"He might get hurt."

"I never did," Chub said. "We'll take it easy."

Bo scowled as if he were getting ready to bang

their heads together, and then he growled, "All right. Just take it easy. Understand?" He stomped away, yelling orders at his logging crew.

"The trouble with him," Chub said, "is he's afraid I'll grow up to be just like him. He's always saying that. He thinks I ought to go to college so I can be a Forest Ranger like Corey."

"I know how that is, Chub. I get the same thing all the time, only it's to be a doctor, and I don't want to be a doctor."

Chub led the way over to the dozer. Having been on the huge one at the sawmill, Briss realized that the machine was not nearly as big as he had thought at first. But when he was on it with Chub, with the engine chugging, he decided it was large enough.

All that morning he rode with Chub, towing logs to the loading machine. Chub explained how all the controls worked, until Briss thought he had everything memorized.

That afternoon, when the men with the chain saws fell behind in their cutting, Briss had his chance. On a fairly level place near the creek,

Chub let Briss get behind the controls.

The first thing Briss did was kill the engine.

"That happens," Chub said. "Start her up and try again."

The engine started easily enough. Dry-mouthed, Briss sat quietly for a moment, feeling the tremendous throbbing power of the machine. "What if I run into something?"

"You won't. Take off!"

Briss took off with a lurch and a grinding roar. He thought he was headed clear off the mountain, but he actually went only a few feet before he remembered to cut down on the throttle. From the edge of the trees, Lassie barked. Briss could not tell whether she was applauding his handling of the dozer, or disapproving his performance.

He made a turn and stopped. "I did it!" he cried.

"Pretty good," Chub said.

Though he was proud of his accomplishment and ready to learn more, Briss remembered his experience with Corey's Jeep. He did not try to rush things. Several times that day and the next he made short runs, gaining a little more confidence in his ability each time.

"In time, you might be pretty good with that," Bo told him, "but I think both of you have had enough for now."

Briss was satisfied. He and Chub went up to the Signal Hill area that day and explored the limestone caves. None of them was very deep, but some were connected so that the boys could go in one place and climb up to emerge at another entrance. Sometimes they had to boost Lassie up steep rises.

They found no Indian skeletons, and both of them were just as happy that they did not. At the end of one of the caves they did find an old canteen with a bullet hole in it. Chub was sure that it must have belonged to some forgotten trapper or mountain man.

Sitting at the mouth of one of the caves, with their feet dangling over the cliff, they ate their lunch and looked out on the great forested sweep of the Sleepy Cat.

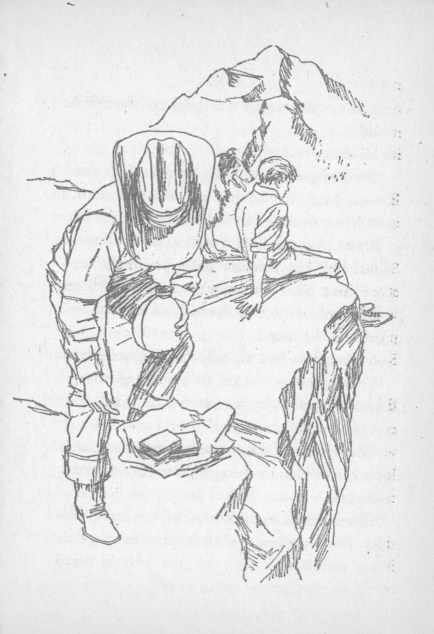

"Boy, there're sure a lot of trees there!" Briss said.

"There wouldn't be, if everybody had gone on cutting them the way they used to. My grandpa was a logger a long time ago. Before he died, he used to rave and snort and tell me how the Forest Service tried to ruin his business. Bo was that way, too, until Corey and him got to be friends."

"You could be a pretty good ranger, I'll bet," Briss said. "Of course, you'd have to learn not to fight all the time."

"I could do that, all right. It's all that book stuff in school that would kill me before I got started." Chub finished the last sandwich. "That wasn't very much lunch, was it?"

As he hiked back to the logging site Briss was glad he had finally changed shoes. He was wearing the new ones that he had bought the day he and Billie had gone to the store. They made walking a lot easier, especially when it came to scrambling over rocks.

The reason he had gotten rid of the cowboy boots

was simple. One morning Corey had told him to do it, and that had settled the problem.

That evening when Briss got back to the ranger station, Corey was talking to a tall, blond man whom he introduced as Bert Stillman.

"Next week I'm going over and inspect Bert's project for a day or two," Corey said. "How would you and Chub like to go along?"

That suited Briss just fine. "Can we camp out?"

"For one night, at least. We can stay at Paywell. It's not bad fishing there, and maybe you can find some more of those bottles, like the one you have in your room."

Briss proudly displayed the canteen he had found almost buried in the sticks and leaves of a rat's nest. Both Corey and Bert Stillman agreed that it was a real old-time object.

During the rest of the week Briss and Chub took several short hikes near the logging site. Lassie was always happy to get away from the sound of the chain saws and the thunder of the heavy equipment. Briss, however, found himself getting very interested in the timber cutting itself.

It was not a haphazard operation, he discovered. Only the older trees were cut, the ones that had been marked for harvesting. "Harvesting" had an odd sound, until he thought about it. He guessed trees were like any crop. You picked what was ripe and let the young plants grow.

He was full of questions. Chub was able to answer some of them, but Briss still had plenty left when he got back to the ranger station every night. He had observed that the tremendous loads of logs brought down each day had all been sliced into lumber by the time Bo and his drivers arrived at the mill the following day with more logs.

Bo seldom delivered any lumber. Trucks came and took it away as fast as he could supply it.

Briss asked Corey about that one night after supper. "You said there were eight sawmills in the Sleepy Cat, and Bo's wasn't even the biggest. With all those mills going, won't you run out of trees someday?"

"That thought came up long ago, when lumber

was about the only product that came from trees. Now we get hundreds of things from wood— phonograph records, sponges, shatterproof glass, and a lot of other things I don't even know about. The demand for wood is greater than ever, and it's going to increase.

"The people who established the Forest Service long ago didn't know what modern science would be doing with wood fifty or a hundred years later, but they did foresee what could happen to our forests if there were no controls over them. Our problems are bigger now, not only to assure a supply of wood for the future, but to maintain forests for recreation, wildlife, and many other uses. We're trying to plan at least two hundred years ahead."

"Two hundred years!" That was too far in the future for Briss to grasp. "You'd better plant a lot of trees."

Corey smiled. "That's part of the answer. Tree farms on private land are a big help, too. I don't think we'll run out of timber, Briss. And you're getting sleepy." Corey pointed. "You know where your bed is."

Waking up in the morning in the cool, pleasant room was something that Briss would never forget. At home he had always been hard to get up, but here he had Lassie to nudge him awake, and he could hear Corey in the kitchen getting breakfast.

He lay for a few moments watching the early sun on the east window. One hand stroked Lassie's silky fur.

The best part of it all was that he had something interesting to do every day.

But something was troubling him a little more each day. He knew he ought to be honest and tell Corey and Sheriff Sam the truth about himself.

The thing was, though, neither his parents nor his grandmother knew he was gone, so they had nothing to worry about. Bobby Crisman, of course . . . well, that was a little different.

While he was dressing, Briss almost decided to tell Corey the truth. And then he had another idea.

On the way to the sawmill that morning to catch his ride with Chub and Bo in the big truck, Briss stopped at a telephone booth in front of an all-night drive-in. He had observed that a lot of boys from the summer camps used that booth. No one would think much about seeing him there.

He called Bobby Crisman's aunt, Mrs. Pascal, in Los Angeles. He tried to make his voice deep.

"Bobby!" she cried. "Where are you?"

"This isn't Bobby, Mrs. Pascal, but he's all right."

"Who is this? Is Bobby with you?"

"He's in a boys' camp. He's all right."

"Who is this? Where—"

"Don't worry about him, Mrs. Pascal. Does his father know that—"

"I can't get in touch with his father. Who—"

Briss hung up. Maybe that would help some, he thought. No one seemed to pay any attention to him as he left the booth and hurried on toward the sawmill with Lassie.

Later that day he told Chub about the call. "I don't know whether that helped or not," Chub said. "If it was me, I'd just tell the truth and wait for somebody to come get me."

"Maybe you wouldn't, either, if you had to live in an apartment, and couldn't go to the Bristlecone Forest, and had a stepmother who took your father off to Europe."

They were sitting on the dozer, waiting for the loggers to trim a felled tree. "What's the matter with your stepmother?" Chub asked. "She's the one you always gripe about."

"Well, she—" Judy was her name. She had not tried to be sticky-sweet with Briss, nor had she been mean, either. She had tried to be friendly. "Oh, she's all right, I guess."

"You don't act like you thought so. What did she do to you?"

"Nothing! I don't have to like her, do I?"

Chub shrugged. "How long have you had her?"

"About two months, I guess. Just long enough to mess up our trip to the Bristlecone Forest."

"Bristlecone! That's all I hear. What's so wonderful about going to see Bristlecones? We've got a place way up above the end of the lake where—"

"I know! And I'm going up there before I leave."

Behind them, one of the loggers shouted, "Are you kids going to argue all day or drag this log to the loader?"

That was the day that Briss realized his ambition to operate the dozer by himself. Late in the afternoon Chub exchanged places with Briss. A heavy log was chained to the tow bar.

"Remember now, you have to give her more power than just running around light," Chub warned.

Briss was doing fine, but it left him a little shaky when, on the way to the loader, Chub suddenly leaped off and left him all by himself. Then he steadied down again and brought the log in just right for the loader to pick up.

"Chub, you knothead!" Bo Wilson roared. "You can get mangled jumping off a moving dozer! That finishes you two. Get out of here, both of you. Go take a hike or something."

"I just wanted to show him he could run it all by himself," Chub protested.

"Yeah, yeah, I know! Beat it, both of you, before you kill yourselves."

They went up the creek a short distance to where a pair of beavers were enlarging their dam. Several times they had watched the beavers in late afternoon. Lassie always cocked her head and whined, acting as if she would like to be friends with the beavers, if they would just give up their silly habit of staying in the water.

"Bo was pretty sore, wasn't he?" Briss said.

"Aw! You ought to see him when he's really mad. He meant it, though, about jumping off that dozer. That was pretty stupid of me." Chub seemed to forget all about it a moment later. "Hey! We get to go camping with Corey day after tomorrow. I've never been to Paywell. We'd better take plenty of grub along."

On the way to Paywell, Briss saw country far different from anything he had seen before in the Sleepy Cat National Forest. This was dry land, with piñons and junipers, rocky hills, and wide, sandy gulches.

Bert Stillman's crew was working in an area of rolling hills and sparse, brown grass. Though Chub and Briss were anxious to get on to Paywell, after they followed Corey and Stillman around for a while, they found themselves interested in the erosion control project.

The land was bone dry now, but there were many small gullies where water had cut down to rock. Along the edges of the channels, the soil was black and deep. All the gullies came together, joining one tremendous wash that was twenty feet deep and fully as wide. In the bottom of it was a trickle of water, green with scum.

"I thought there was a creek over here," Chub said.

"When it rains, there's quite a bit more than a creek here," Stillman said.

Looking down into the big gully, Chub shook his head.

"Don't worry, we'll find more water," Corey said. He looked at Stillman. "I'll bet these boys won't believe that a fair-sized trout stream ran through here eighty years ago, with willows and beaver dams and grass all along the edges."

"Where'd it go?" Chub asked. "I mean, what happened?"

"A lot of things. The grass was over-grazed so that the rains started to run off and carry soil away. All the ponderosa was logged out of here for mine timbers, and that helped to start erosion." Corey pointed at the deep gully. "That was a road once."

"Down in that hole?" Chub asked doubtfully.

Stillman laughed. "No. Right on top. Wagon wheels rutted it out, water began to run down it, and when it got bad in one place, the wagons moved over a little and started more erosion. Now the thing is a baby Grand Canyon."

Briss had been studying the work that was going on. The men and the machines were not doing anything at all in the main gully, but on the feeder channels that came down to it they were building small rock dams. Out from both sides of the dams they were blading ditches to carry the overflow water along the hills on a gentle grade.

Pretty smart, he thought, and really quite simple, too. But what about that tremendous washout that used to be a road? He knew it ran all the way to the highway.

"These boys are itching to get on and set up camp," Corey told Stillman. "I'll be back this afternoon, and I'll be here all day tomorrow."

Lassie preferred to run the rest of the way to Paywell. What was left of the old road was so rough that Corey had to creep along, and that gave

Lassie plenty of time to explore off to the sides of the road. Sometimes she stopped ahead of them to wait for the Jeep to catch up.

As Corey had said, they found more water the higher they went. They crawled to the top of a steep hill, and there below them in a wide, grassy flat sat the mining camp. Briss saw the shine of a beaver pond not far from the crumbling buildings.

"Boy, what a place to explore!" Chub cried. "I'll bet we can find all kinds of stuff there."

"I don't doubt that," Corey said, "but I wouldn't guarantee the kind of stuff it will be."

"Bottles," Briss said. "I want purple bottles."

"I want pieces of gold that somebody lost," Chub said.

Both boys were excited and happy as they helped Corey set up the tent on a high place near one of the buildings.

"Why do we even need a tent?" Chub asked. "It hasn't rained since that day we were looking for the Road Hog."

"If you don't have one, it will," Corey said. He

ate lunch with them, and then he said, "I want you to stick right here in the town while I'm gone. Okay?"

"Okay," they agreed.

"Watch where you step when you fool around those old buildings. There're nails sticking up in all those boards. Lassie, you stay here with the boys."

Lassie's attitude said she had already made that decision.

After Corey left, Chub insisted that fishing should come first. It was easy to run out of food, he said, and that would be a terrible thing.

"You fish; I'll look for bottles," Briss said.

Now and then as he kicked around among tin cans and the scattered trash of the old camp, Briss heard Chub let out a big whoop. Chub was standing on a rock below the beaver dam, throwing his hook up and over the tangle of aspen logs. He was catching fish, sure enough.

Bottle-hunting was not so good. Briss found plenty of broken glass, some of it beautiful purple, but no sound bottles. There had to be some around, he was sure, for it did not appear that many people ever came to Paywell.

It was not long before Chub came over to where Briss was rooting in a pile of cans. Lassie was helping a little, pawing at the ground, though she did not seem to understand the object of the search.

"I got enough fish for supper," Chub said. "They're all cleaned and put away in a cool place. What are you finding?"

"Nothing but busted glass."

"What do you expect? All kinds of people have tramped around here. You've got to dig. Why, some of those tourists around Big Sunset bring rakes with them when they go looking for bottles." From a collapsed building Chub took a narrow board. He drove four nails through one end of it. "There!"

Using the tool, Briss found it easy to rake down through the topsoil and pine needles and leaves to where the trash was undisturbed. "Hey!" he yelled when he discovered a square, unbroken bottle.

He ran to the creek to wash it, and Lassie went along to share in the excitement. With some of the dirt washed off, the bottle showed a deep purple color when Briss held it to the sun.

"That *is* kind of pretty," Chub admitted. He made another rake. Working together, the boys found six more good bottles in the same trash pile. "You can have them all," Chub offered. "We've got lots of time to be garbage diggers, though, so right now let's go look at some of these old buildings."

Briss was willing. Now that Chub had showed him how to find bottles, he knew he could return to the search anytime.

In the ruined buildings Lassie chased rats, while Briss and Chub poked into odd corners in search of anything interesting. Chub still had it in his head that there ought to be some gold coins lying around.

"Why would there be?" Briss asked. "Nobody throws money around on the floor."

"Maybe somebody had a hole in his pocket."

They found a variety of interesting things—four teakettles with holes in the bottom, a miner's candlestick, a block plane, and three burro shoes. But they did not find any gold. Chub then confessed that his idea was based on the fact that a boy he knew in Big Sunset had found a tobacco can with three hundred dollars in gold coins in a mining camp on the other side of the range. "I guess these guys over here spent everything they had," Chub said disgustedly.

The afternoon was gone before the boys realized it. When they heard Corey's Jeep returning, they tramped back to the camp with their loot.

"Let's see that square teakettle, Chub," Corey said.

"It leaks just like the others. We're going to throw them all away."

Corey examined the utensil carefully. "Don't throw this one away. It's handmade copper. I've never seen anything like it."

Chub perked up. "Valuable, huh?"

"I wouldn't say that, but at one of those antique

shops in Big Sunset, it would probably be priced at twenty-five bucks. You wouldn't get that much for it, of course."

"I'll take five bucks!" Chub changed his mind quickly. "No, I won't. I'll give it to Billie Sanderson. She's nuts about old junk like that."

Corey grinned. "That wouldn't have anything to do with the fact that her husband is one of your teachers?"

"That's an idea!" Chub said. "It won't hurt me. Mr. Sanderson sort of goes for old junk, too."

Briss knew Corey was a good cook, but he seemed to outdo himself that evening. For once, Briss ate about as much as Chub consumed. Just being outside with two good friends had a lot to do with it, Briss guessed. Sunset glow was on the beaver pond, where fish were rising. The little valley was peaceful and quiet. For a while Briss could believe that there was no one else in the world but the three of them and Lassie.

I want to spend a lot of time in places like this, he thought. *And I'm going to do it, too.* He guessed he must have known that from his very first visit with his father to the Bristlecone Forest in California.

"No one owns Paywell, do they?" Chub asked.

"All this area reverted to the Forest Service a long time ago," Corey explained. "We have a campground planned for here sometime in the next five years."

"Boy, that'll sure ruin the fishing!"

"For the people who come here now—maybe forty during the whole summer. With a road and a campground, thousands will be able to enjoy this place."

"Not me," Chub said, "not when it gets that crowded."

"We'll still have wilderness areas for people-haters like you, Chub." Corey winked at Briss.

"I don't hate people," Chub protested. "I just don't want to trip over them when I go out in the mountains."

"That's what wilderness areas are for," Corey said. "Not only for people who want to get away from it all for a while, but also for thousands who will never actually get to a wilderness area."

"I don't get it." Chub frowned. "If people never go to a place, what good is it to them?"

"Just knowing that wide-open spaces still exist in America can be a great satisfaction to people." Corey saw doubt still in Chub's expression. "Bo tells me you've been saving most of the money he pays you for helping him."

"Sure. He wants me to go to college someday."

"Do you know how much you've saved?"

"About, I guess."

"Do you go down to the bank and count it every day?"

"Naw! I know it's there, and someday I can use it if I want to. It makes me feel pretty good just to know—" Chub stopped suddenly. "Yeah, I get what you mean, Corey!"

Sitting with Lassie at his feet, Briss had been following the conversation closely. He knew what Corey meant. Briss remembered all the maps and other stuff he had gotten from the Forest Service.

Sometimes when he should have been studying, he had pored over the material in his room, reading about wild places, dreaming over the pictures.

At first he had not thought he would ever get to go to any of the places, but in his mind he could visit them, and it made him feel good just to know that there were great, wild areas in America that would always be kept that way. It would have been an awful feeling to know that in the whole country there was no place less crowded than a city.

"I get the idea," Chub said to Corey, "but I still say it's better to go than just to think about going."

"I wouldn't disagree." Corey rose. "Let's clean up the camp."

Chub helped with the dishes, while Briss, with some help from Lassie, dug a garbage pit. The shovel sliced through sod with thick grass roots, and that caused him to wonder about the washed-out area below Paywell. When he returned to the fire he asked, "Why wouldn't a lot of dams across that big gully be a good thing?"

"They would be all right," Corey said, "until

they filled up with water during a heavy rain. Unless you had expensive dams, the water would cut around the ends and start new erosion. We're trying to stop the erosion where it begins, and that means in all those little feeders that supply the main gully.

"By distributing the water out from those small erosion cuts, we choke off the big gully. Then the little scars begin to heal over with grass, and the lateral ditches let water soak away slowly so more grass can grow on the hills. In just a year's time you will see a tremendous change beginning down there."

"But that great big gully," Chub said. "What happens to it?"

"In time the banks round out, grass takes hold, and the gully slowly turns into a swale, instead of a flood channel," Corey explained.

"Will it ever fill up?" Briss asked.

"It took about eighty years to get like it is. Maybe in three hundred years it won't be so noticeable."

Chub grinned. "We'll all be pretty old by then."

Both boys kept Corey busy answering questions until after dark, and then they fell into long periods of silence.

This was one of the best parts of camping, Briss thought, just sitting around a campfire with people you liked, and thinking about what you were going to do the next day.

Briss was thinking ahead a little farther than the next day, however. He was getting closer to telling the truth about himself, but he had not decided just when to do it.

They had been quiet for a long time. Then Corey said, "Briss, you must have told Chub about yourself, haven't you?"

Startled, the boys looked at each other quickly.

"Yes," Briss said.

"But I can't tell you," Chub added quickly.

"No one asked you to, Chub." Corey yawned. "How many, besides me, are ready for bed?"

They were in the tent in their sleeping bags when Briss asked, "Corey, can Chub and I go to the Bristlecone place?"

Corey did not answer right away. "That depends on what the sheriff has to say when we get back. If he okays it, it will be all right with me. I'm going up that way in a few days to look at the road."

"We want to camp out," Chub said.

"I assumed as much. Now go to sleep."

CHUB'S FIRST comment when he saw the squat, twisted trees was, "They sure wouldn't be much good for lumber."

"Lumber!" Briss was horrified. "No one is ever going to cut these trees for anything!"

"Okay, Ranger Russell. Don't get so excited," Chub said good-naturedly.

Ranger Russell. That had a fine sound, Briss thought.

They were high on a windy point, two miles from their camp at the lake. The forest was not nearly as large as the one in California, Briss observed, but the Bristlecones were the same, sculptured by wind and ice, thousands of years old, and still clinging sturdily to life.

Their age alone made them something special

to Briss, but it was the way they had survived that impressed him most. As he and Chub wandered over the dry hills Briss pointed out trees still alive that had been burned by fire centuries before.

In one narrow saddle between the hills, where even the rocks had been etched by wind and snow and ice, they found a Bristlecone that lay almost parallel to the ground. Its stubby branches still bore needles and deep purple cones.

"Boy, these things are tough!" Chub said. "They don't give up, no matter what." Before the day was over, he was as much impressed as Briss by the sturdy independence of the Bristlecone Pines.

Oddly, when they returned to their camp that day Briss felt that he had seen enough. Suddenly he was anxious to tell Sheriff Sam and Corey the truth. When he had been planning to run away from home he had told himself that it was because he had to go to see the Bristlecones again.

But now he knew his running away really had been caused by a desire to hurt his father and Judy for leaving him alone, for ruining his trip to the

Inyo Forest. Worst of all, he had gotten Bobby Crisman mixed up in the mess, and now, in spite of Briss's phone call to Bobby's aunt, Bobby's folks were probably worrying their heads off about him.

"The first thing I'm going to do when Corey comes after us day after tomorrow is—" Briss stopped as Lassie began to bark.

She was looking down the road. A few moments later the boys heard the sound of a hard-working automobile.

The Iowa car that soon pulled in was towing a trailer with a small boat. After the driver stopped near the lake, a man and a woman and three small girls got out.

"How do you like that?" Chub said disgustedly. "No matter how far away you get, even in a Jeep—"

"They have a right here, Chub. Let's go talk to them."

The woman was admiring Lassie as the boys walked down to the lake.

"You boys come up by boat, did you?" the man asked.

"No, sir," Briss answered. "We came up with the Forest Ranger."

"It looks like the Forest Service could do a better job of building a road in here," the man complained. "I would have turned back, but after I got into the worst of it, I couldn't do anything but keep going." He looked at his boat. "I'll never be able to pull that back up some of those hills."

"The Forest Service didn't build that road," Chub said. "It's an old one that people got started to using." He looked over the boat with interest. "That's a nice outboard motor. You want us to help you put her in the lake?"

"I may as well use it while I'm here."

With Briss's and Chub's help, the man got his boat in the water. He seemed to feel better then. "Maybe I can get back up those steep hills by taking a run at them."

Briss saw a grin on Chub's face when they went back to their own camp near a little stream. "If we work it right, that man will let us run his boat down the lake to Big Sunset."

The idea appealed to Briss, but he said, "Huh-uh, Chub! Corey wouldn't know where we were. We got into that before, when we went up the mountain with those Red Devils. Maybe that turned out all right, but I'm not going to get into another mess."

"We could go down real early, before Corey started to come up in the Jeep. Then he wouldn't have to make the trip at all."

"No, Chub. Something might happen, and Corey wouldn't have any idea where we were."

"Are you afraid of the water, Briss?"

"No! I went across from Rocky Beach to the other side on a raft I built myself, didn't I?"

Chub nodded. "I guess you're right. I don't want to mess things up with Corey, either. Besides, the man didn't say we could run his boat to Big Sunset. He thinks he can pull it out of here, but I'll bet he can't."

The visitors were in bed early that night.

Briss and Chub and Lassie stayed up about two hours later, just sitting around the fire.

"You know something, Chub? I've got two things to tell Corey. First, who I am. Second, that I'm going to be a ranger."

"I knew that last thing all along."

"How did you know?" Briss asked.

"Anyone could tell that, from the way you always talk about trees and things, and all those questions you ask Corey all the time. I thought you never would stop talking about that erosion stuff over at Paywell."

"You asked a few questions yourself, Chub."

Chub grinned. "Didn't I, though? I like the part about trees. I really like that. This stuff about planting grass, or telling ranchers where to put their cows—there isn't much to that."

"You could be a forester."

"That's what Bo keeps telling me. He's made me save my money to go to college, but I don't know. I'm pretty dumb in school."

"That's what *you* say! Billie Sanderson says her

husband told her you were plenty smart, when you wanted to be. You just like to goof off."

"That's right. I know it." The firelight was strong on Chub's round face as he stared into the flames.

"We could go to college together, Chub. We could go to the same one where Corey went. He's told me about it." Briss was excited and eager to make his point.

"Hey! That sounds all right. Maybe I could play football, too. If I'm as big as Bo when I grow up, and half as tough, I could play football pretty good."

Now they were both excited about the idea of going to college together to become rangers. Chub made his decision. "I'll do it, if we can go together." They shook hands on it to seal the solemn vow.

When they got into their sleeping bags in the tiny tent a short time later, they were still talking over their plans. Lassie curled up at their feet and let out a big sigh, as if wishing they would be quiet so she could sleep.

Briss was prepared now to take the first big step toward the future. As soon as possible he was going to tell Corey and Sheriff Sam the complete truth.

He went to sleep wishing that Corey were coming after them the next day, instead of the day after that.

The popping sound of an outboard motor roused them. They crawled out of their tent, yawning and blinking, to find that the other campers were already up and about. The Iowa man was just going out on the lake.

"Boy, he's sure an early bird," Chub said. "He'd better watch out what he's doing, too. That shallow bay out there is nothing but stumps and rocks."

Lassie was sitting on the shore, watching the boater. She came back to the camp when the man killed his engine and began to fish.

After breakfast Briss asked, "What do you want to do today?"

"I want to go back and look at the Bristlecones, of course. That's why we came up here."

The visit the day before to the Bristlecones had done something for Briss that he did not quite understand. It was as if he had completed a mission and no longer needed to fret about it. He would have preferred to hike around the lake that day. "Okay with me, Ranger Wilson."

Once they were back among the Bristlecones, Briss was glad they had made the second trip. He explained to Chub how scientists had taken core drillings of the trees in the Bristlecone Forest of California.

"It doesn't hurt the tree, but still they can read all the rings and tell how old the tree is, and when there were dry spells, or fires, or lots of rain. They can get the whole history of the trees that way. Take Methuselah, forty-six hundred years old. Think of what's happened in the world since that one popped up from a seed!"

It was still the tough independence of the trees that impressed Chub most. They stood beside a gnarled old Bristlecone that had only a small part of its bark left. Most of the trunk seemed to be completely dead, but there were still green branches in the stubby top.

Chub spread his arms to measure the diameter of the trunk. "You say it grows less than an inch in diameter every one hundred years?"

"That's what the rangers in Inyo told me."

They sat with their backs to one of the Bristlecones as they ate their lunch. It had been a warm, sunny morning, but now clouds were gathering on the mountains, and there was a dampness in the air.

"It looks like that day when we were searching for Road Hog," Briss commented. "Only worse."

"We can really get gully-busters here, when we do get rain," Chub said. "We'd better get back to camp fast."

The rain caught them when they were still a half mile from their camp. The lake below became white with the seething downpour. Lassie tucked in her tail and ran with them as they plunged downhill. Soaked to the skin, they crawled inside the tent.

They had stowed everything inside but their cooking utensils. Outside, the rain rattled the lid of a pot and made a drumming sound on the frying pan.

Briss dug in his pack for a change of clothes. Severe as the rain was, it could not last forever, he knew. "You'd better get into some dry clothes, Chub."

Chub had rolled his sleeping bag back and was lying on the ground cloth. Suddenly he crawled outside. Briss heard him vomiting. When Chub came back, he was shivering and his face was pale. He flopped down again.

"What's the matter, Chub?"

"I don't know. I got to feeling bad just after we started down. My stomach, I guess." Chub crossed his hands on his chest. He was shaking. "I'll be all right in a minute."

He was not all right in a minute, nor in twenty minutes. He had to keep going outside in the rain, though there was nothing left in his stomach after the first two times. Chub tried to grin, but it was a wan expression. "I'm sick, I guess."

There was no guess about it, Briss thought. He was awful sick. "I'll take you down to those Iowa people and—"

"They're gone," Chub said. "I didn't notice that, either, until a minute ago. The boat's still there, though." He wiped his lips. "Will you get me some water?"

The water did not stay down very long.

Briss was scared clear through. It was fourteen miles back to the highway. Corey was not due until the next day. As sick as Chub was, Briss knew he had to get him to a doctor as quickly as possible. But how?

The rain was coming down worse than ever.

Water was striking the Jeep windshield so fast that the wiper blades could scarcely handle it, but Corey could see ahead well enough to know that he had started too late.

Ten feet of muddy water, carrying dead wood and pine needles, was boiling down the gulch just ahead. He was only four miles from the highway. There were five or six more gulches like this one between him and where he had left Briss and Chub.

They would be all right, he was sure. All they had to do was wait out the rain. Tomorrow they would start walking back to the highway, for Chub, certainly, would realize what the rain had done to the old road.

As Corey was backing up to turn around, Billie called on the radio. "The sheriff has confirmation. He's David Brian Russell, sure enough. It seems that he pulled a switch at the bus station and sent the other boy to camp in his place."

It had taken time, but with Sheriff Sam patiently putting many little pieces together, the mystery of young Bristlecone had been solved. "I'm turning back now," Corey said. "I made it only about four miles off the highway. Has the sheriff notified the parents?"

"They're out of the country, but he did talk to Briss's grandmother."

The rain had stopped by the time Corey reached

the highway, but it was only a brief respite. It was pouring again when he went over Twenty-Mile Bridge. Something kept pecking at his mind.

Going in, he had met an Iowa car with a light boat trailer. The man had seen the cloud buildup and had gotten out as fast as he could, leaving his boat behind, Corey realized.

Both Briss and Chub were adventurous kids. While Corey was sure they would not panic just because of a heavy rain, he wondered if they would get ideas about that outboard left so handily near their camp.

There was another short lull in the rain, when it seemed that it might be ending, but then it started once more.

At the Thunder Narrows road, Corey pulled off and called his office to tell Billie where he would be until dark.

"The way it's raining, it's almost dark now," Billie said.

THEY LEFT DURING the second lull in the rain. Chub was so sick he could hardly walk, but he made it down to the boat. Briss threw in the tent, and then he helped Chub over the side, folding part of the canvas under him and the rest over him.

Chub had to tell him how to start the outboard.

"Go as slow as she'll run for a ways. If you hit the prop on a stump or rock, we're done."

Briss did his best to follow Chub's advice. He kept the speed of the boat down as low as possible, and watched for obstacles. Sometimes he had to grab the oar to fend off from stumps at water level. Three times he scraped rocks with the hull; he held his breath until the boat grated clear.

They reached deeper water just as the rain came slashing in again.

The wind was raising whitecaps that slopped into the boat. Chub crawled past Lassie toward the bailing bucket.

"Stay in the middle," he groaned, "and head straight into the chops. You're doing fine." Then he collapsed on the bottom of the boat.

New fear swept through Briss. He did not think he was doing very well. With the rain and the wind-driven lake water beating his face, he sometimes could not see anything ahead but seething froth. He did his best to steer the boat into the whitecaps. The bow kept slapping up and down ominously.

Chub opened his eyes. "Gun it," he said. "You've got to keep the back end down."

When Briss gave the motor more gas, the bow of the little boat slapped all the harder, but the stern stayed down and they kept moving. Chub, his face pale and strained, rose up, gritted his teeth, and tried to bail.

Lassie was crouched down forward. She whined as she turned to look back at the boys. Her long fur was plastered to her body, and water was streaming off her nose.

Briss could see the shore only dimly. He wanted to go in, but he knew he had to keep pounding ahead until they reached some place where he could get help for Chub.

The motor sputtered. Briss felt his heart jump. And then the motor caught again and went on strongly.

On hands and knees, Chub raised his head weakly. It took all his strength to raise the bailing bucket. A gust of wind caught them broadside, and the boat yawed. Chub was thrown against the side. Grabbing for support, his hand thumped a red gasoline can strapped to the side.

When the boat steadied, Chub reached out and thumped the can again. Briss, glancing at him, saw a look of hopelessness cross his face.

"Empty?" asked Briss.

Chub nodded weakly.

"We'll go as far as we can!" Briss shouted. He hoped there was enough gas in the tank to take them to the marina. Or maybe the gas would last long enough for them to meet a big boat that could take Chub aboard and take the little outboard in tow.

But as he looked at the rough water Briss knew they were not likely to meet any boat.

He recognized Thunder Narrows on his right. Waves were churning against the rocky beach, and the cliffs above looked twice as tall as he remembered.

The motor did not even sputter when it quit. One moment it was churning, and a moment later it was dead.

And then they were adrift in the choppy water. Waves began to spill over the bow, slopping into the boat. In desperation Briss pulled the starter rope, but the motor did not respond.

"Out of gas," Chub gasped. He pulled himself up to look toward the beach.

Briss grabbed the oar. The wind pushed the bow around. No matter on which side he paddled, he did not seem to be getting anywhere. It was not far to shore. He could see driftwood piled in the rocks, and more of it sloshing back and forth on the beach.

It seemed to him that the boat ought to drift in, like the logs, and then he realized that it was the wind against the boat that was defeating him. But, paddling with all his strength, he did get closer.

And then a blast of wind spun the boat and it began to go the wrong way.

Neither Chub nor Briss saw the man who was plunging down the slippery trail from the top of the cliffs. The man had a rope.

It was Corey. He knew the rope was too short, but it was all he could do.

Briss saw a light line strung back and forth on cleats. He scrambled forward and began to unwind it. He tied four knots in one end, around each other, any way he could put them together hastily to make bulk.

"Lassie, here!"

For a moment Briss was afraid he could not

make her understand, and then Lassie took the rope end in her mouth.

"Swim, Lassie! Take it ashore!"

The boat rocked as he pushed her toward the side.

Lassie understood. She knew something was wrong, and she could see the shore. In a scrambling leap she went over the side. Briss could see just her head as the whitecaps rolled over her.

He played out the line carefully. Too much would drag her down in the water, while not enough would keep her from making progress.

Sometimes he could not see her at all. Then her head would appear in the wild water. Lassie was fighting a gallant battle to get ashore with the line.

It looked as if she was going to make it.

Then the rope ran out in Briss's hands. He was down to the end of it, and Lassie was still some distance from the beach.

The gallant dog would not give up, however. She tried to take the line on in, but now she had

the weight of the drifting boat against her. She went under twice. She came up still fighting, still holding the line, but she was weakening.

She would drown before she gave up, Briss knew.

He was ready to let the rope go. And then he saw Corey lunging out into the water. He, too, had a rope. He tied it to a jutting rock, and then he swam toward the struggling Lassie.

When he reached her he sent her on ashore, and then he tied his rope to the one she had been tugging. It was no problem then for Briss, crouched in the bow of the little boat, to pull into the beach.

Now that they were safe, Corey was mad clear through. He started to say something in anger, and then he had a close look at Chub. "Are you hurt?"

"He's sick to his stomach something awful," Briss said. "That's why we tried to come down in the boat."

Corey asked no more questions. He picked Chub up in his arms. "Pull that boat high on the beach, Briss." And then Corey started up the steep trail.

Lassie had been lying down, panting. She had recovered enough to shake vigorously and trot away with Briss when he followed Corey.

Briss had five more days in Big Sunset. He spent two of them worrying about Chub and visiting him at the clinic.

Dr. Nye laid Chub's trouble to a mayonnaise sandwich. "The things you kids put in your stomachs!" Dr. Nye shook his head. "Mayonnaise belongs in a refrigerator, not on a camping trip."

"I kept it in a cold stream," Chub said weakly.

"Then you smeared it on bread and carried it half a day in a hot pack. If you had been a few more hours getting here, it might have been too late."

As it was, Dr. Nye let Chub out of the clinic on the evening of the second day. Chub did not look too frisky, but his grin was back.

"If it wasn't for Lassie, you wouldn't even be alive," Bo Wilson growled. He had sat all night beside Chub's bed after Corey brought him to the clinic, but now that Chub was all right, Bo could afford to act tough again.

Briss now had three days left before his father would arrive by plane to take him home. Mr. Russell had returned a week early from Europe, even before he knew Briss was missing. From the sheriff's office Briss had talked to him by telephone.

After he hung up, Briss had found it difficult to keep from crying. In fact, he did wipe a few tears away quickly, while Sheriff Sam sat quietly, watching him.

"When you get back home, Briss," the sheriff said, "I'll bet you'll discover that your father has got a lot smarter than you thought he was."

It was a left-handed way of putting it, but Briss understood what Sheriff Sam meant.

The sheriff knew everything about him now. Briss had told Corey the truth while they were rushing Chub to the clinic. Afterward they went to the courthouse, where Briss repeated everything for Sheriff Sam.

Briss was very glad of one thing: He had made his confession *before* he knew that the sheriff already had all the basic facts.

Mr. Russell arrived three hours earlier than expected. Briss and Chub were just finishing lunch with Corey in the ranger's kitchen. They had seen the green and white plane go over, but a lot of light planes came and went at the Big Sunset airport, so they had paid no particular attention to this one.

Anyway, Briss's father was not due to arrive until much later that afternoon.

Briss went to the door to let Lassie out. He saw the car pull in at the ranger station. He saw the tall, dark-haired man who got out of it.

And then Briss went running toward his father.

Chub knocked his chair over as he jumped to the door to see what was happening. "They're sure glad to see each other," he reported. "Hey, Corey, Mr. Russell looks kind of young. I'll bet he could walk pretty good in the mountains."

Corey smiled. "Oh, that's a fine qualification

for a father, Chub. You can always tell a good one that way."

"What I mean is, he doesn't look like someone who would go running off to Europe to look at crummy old palaces and stuff, when he could have had a lot more fun camping out with me and Briss."

"Maybe you ought to tell him that, Chub."

"Maybe I just will."

Chub did not get around to it, however. After Briss brought his father up to the house, Chub found himself pretty well taken with Mr. Russell. For one thing, Briss's father was a pretty good listener. He did not ask a lot of silly questions while Corey was telling him about his son's experiences around Big Sunset.

Another point in his favor, Chub thought, was that he seemed to like Corey from the very first.

After he had heard the story, Mr. Russell thanked Corey for what he had done for Briss. And then he said, "Later this summer I plan to come back here with David—I mean *Briss*—for a week."

"That's great!" Chub cried. He had not had much chance to break into the conversation. "We can show you all kinds of places to go."

"You're both welcome to stay here with me." Corey rose. "Come on, Chub; let's go see how the office is doing."

For more than an hour Briss and his father stayed in Corey's house. Chub hung around the office. "Why do they have to talk so long?" he asked Billie.

"They probably have a few things to work out."

"I don't know what. Mr. Russell wasn't mad, or anything like that."

Billie smiled. "Go pester Corey for a while, will you? I have work to do."

"What do you think I have?" Corey called from his office. He was sitting at his desk grinning when Chub came in. "If you had run off, Chub, don't you suppose Bo would have a few things to say to you when he found you?"

"Boy, would he! You could hear him clear down on the lake." Chub shook his head at the papers on Corey's desk. "When me and Briss get to be rangers, we're going to change that kind of stuff."

"I hope you can." Corey paused. "You and Briss are going to be rangers?"

"We made our minds up, and we're not fooling."

Mr. Russell confirmed the seriousness of the boys' plans when he came in a little later. He talked to Corey while Briss and Chub and Lassie stayed in the yard.

"I believe Briss and I have come to a rather solid understanding, Mr. Stuart. The trouble seems to have stemmed from my marriage, after Briss's mother died. I think we can iron out our problems there, too."

"I'm glad to hear it," Corey said.

"Briss is determined to be a Forest Ranger. I'm sure you know that."

"No, I did not, but Chub just now told me."

"That Chub seems to be quite a lad himself." Mr. Russell frowned. "To tell the truth, I had something else in mind for Briss, but if he wants to be in the Forest Service. . . . What's your reaction to that, Mr. Stuart? Is there some hero worship involved?"

Corey studied Mr. Russell carefully. "I'd be lying if I said no, but I don't think it was a major force in their decision. Both of those boys are really interested in Forest Service problems. We need the kind of men they're going to be."

Mr. Russell nodded. "If Briss still feels the way he does now when the time comes for college, I'll see that he gets what he wants." He turned toward the door. "I want to see the sheriff now. From what Briss has told me of him, he's a man I'd like to meet. And I want to see Bo Wilson, too, and thank him."

Sitting beside his father in the green and white plane as they lifted into the early-morning air the next day, Briss waved his hand across the window, looking down at his friends.

They were waving, too—Chub and Corey, Sheriff Sam and big Bo Wilson. And Lassie was there, looking up at the plane.

Briss swallowed hard as the figures on the ground grew smaller.

"We'll be back," his father said. "Not only later this summer, Briss, but for a good many more summers to come."

YOU WILL ENJOY

THE TRIXIE BELDEN SERIES

22 Exciting Titles

THE MEG MYSTERIES

6 Baffling Adventures

ALSO AVAILABLE

Algonquin
Alice in Wonderland
A Batch of the Best
More of the Best
Still More of the Best
Black Beauty
The Call of the Wild
Dr. Jekyll and Mr. Hyde
Frankenstein
Golden Prize
Gypsy from Nowhere
Gypsy and Nimblefoot
Lassie—Lost in the Snow
Lassie—The Mystery of Bristlecone Pine
Lassie—The Secret of the Smelters' Cave
Lassie—Trouble at Panter's Lake
Match Point
Seven Great Detective Stories
Sherlock Holmes
Shudders
Tales of Time and Space
Tee-Bo and the Persnickety Prowler
Tee-Bo in the Great Hort Hunt
That's Our Cleo
The War of the Worlds
The Wonderful Wizard of Oz